Hang Him When He Is Not There

T0108036

HANG HIM

when

HE IS NOT THERE

Nicholas John Turner

ZEROGRAM
PRESS

Los Angeles, CA 2021

ZEROGRAM PRESS
1147 El Medio Ave.
Pacific Palisades, CA 90272
EMAIL: info@zerogrampress.com
WEBSITE: www.zerogrampress.com

Distributed by Small Press United / Independent Publishers Group
(800) 888-4741 / www.ipgbook.com

First Zerogram Press Edition 2021
Copyright © 2021 by Nicholas John Turner
Originally published in 2018 by Splice (UK)
All rights reserved

Cover photo by Boone Studios
Book design by Pablo Capra

LIBRARY OF CONGRESS CATALOGING-IN-PUBLICATION DATA

Names: Turner, Nicholas John, author.
Title: Hang him when he is not there / Nicholas John Turner.
Description: First Zerogram Press edition. | Los Angeles, CA : Zerogram Press,
    2021.
Identifiers: LCCN 2020043729 | ISBN 9781953409003 (paperback)
Subjects: LCGFT: Short stories.
Classification: LCC PR9619.4.T876 H36 2021 | DDC 823/.92--dc23
LC record available at https://lccn.loc.gov/2020043729

Printed in the United States of America

NOW I'M FOR SURE going to struggle to explain the way she just sat there, okay. So just you try to be patient now because I do have something to say here and you might be glad you listened. The thing is that it's not like she was an athlete before. What's an athlete, you're asking? Athlete's what we call the ones that have enough steam left in them to try and get out the gates now and then. Do the bolt. Head off down the hill. To home I guess. But that's not what I'm saying about this one so don't be confused. This one was never any trouble. Not capable of it. By the look on her face if you'd asked me six months ago I'd have said without a doubt that she was stuck in the last room, if you know what I mean. I've seen it a thousand times, the same look, like they've been walking forever through some mansion that's always had a million hallways and rooms and attics and dungeons, and they've always just without really knowing why been going through this doorway or up that stairwell, not really chasing anything in particular, just moving from place to place, and now suddenly for the first time they're standing in a room that doesn't seem to have any way in or out, no doors or passages, not even the one they came through to get there, and so they just stand there, or sometimes I guess they sit, with that face I'm telling you about, which is pretty hard to explain in any other way. You've really got to describe it by saying what it's not, if you know what I mean. Nursing homes are God's waiting room, that's what they say and it's pretty well right bang on the money. Anyhow, I'd seen her standing around and I know that look that I've been explaining like the back of my hand. That was before. And so now she'd given up with the standing and instead she sat there, right. Nothing special in it, maybe, and especially if you're thinking that she's just faded away a little more. A natural progression I guess from standing to sitting to being six feet under if you'll excuse me for saying it like that. You get desensitised. Anyway excuse me. The thing about it that I'm trying to explain is that now she *wasn't* blank in the way she was before that I been describing. Not since the incident. She'd kind of gone backwards in that regard, which is something I'd never seen before, or I don't think I have. She *wasn't* in that last room anymore. I mean because don't be mistaken and think that this last room I'm talking about is just some place you get to when you're real close to being dead, like when people talk about seeing a white light or whatever. Because that's a kind of hopeful thing, that light, and plenty of people end up making it back from there and telling the story and that's why we all know about it. But you don't ever hear anything about the last room and you can only really guess what it's like by looking at a lot of people that find themselves in there. The last room's like the place you get to by your *own* walking, and no-one bangs on the walls or screams for help. When you're there you know you belong there if you know what I mean. It's hard to explain, obviously. Anyway the point is that she was in there and then she wasn't, and that's not something I've ever seen in thirty-seven years watching these folks come and go. It's always a one-way trip you know. I mean one day this lady's standing around in all parts of the house with a look on her face that's usually the last look you ever get like I've been saying. And the next she's sitting down by the window and staring out and even though she isn't smiling or moving or looking like she's able to make sense of things, her face is more, damn it, what's the word. It's like her face had changed in a way that you couldn't put your finger on or describe. You know like when someone gets a bit of bad news and their face doesn't really change but just sort of stops. Or when someone looks happy even though they aren't smiling. *Animated*, that's the word. So this old bird's face wasn't changed or anything, just reanimated. Like there was something behind it again. She had this look on her face of confidence or something. *Arrogance* maybe. No, not that. *Confidence*? I don't know. And even though she was pretty well cactus by then, and I don't reckon she could move by herself anymore, she looked like she knew exactly what she was doing again, if you know what I mean. Whereas before she was in that last room, as I've said or tried to anyway. I know it isn't helping but the last room is the only way I know to say what I'm saying. And I guess I never took much notice but some of the nurses I've spoken to even reckon she used to carry a book around back then just to hide the fact that she'd lost it. And thinking back I guess that might be right. Women are funny like that. Full of vanity, until the last. They reckon she was carrying it around for three years, the very same book, and anyway probably she couldn't even read anymore, and I guess she was really just holding up the book like a mask or something so no-one could see she was stuck you know where and probably a little ashamed of it. But now since the incident she'd gotten rid of the book and was just sitting there looking... you know, *confidence* isn't the word either. I knew I was gonna get caught up on this. That look on her face, sitting there, hands in her lap, looking out over the lawns or something at something maybe just down the hill that she couldn't see yet, like she was waiting for a bus or something. Like she was just waiting for something that whatever it was was definitely coming and couldn't have been far off either. I never seen it like that before, I tell you.

1

(AH, I REMEMBER WHY I was listening now; there was news of the avalanche in New Zealand. The survivors were speaking, for the first time, of their lives under the snow; they were reverent, of the nature that swarmed them, and the humanity that saved them. Everything, they said, felt in balance. They were swollen with awe. And I thought of my father, who people always said used to come at you like an avalanche, whether it was just to shake your hand in the street or to crush you on the field. He was a giant, a thin-blooded Maori with a curly silver moustache and eyes that sloped away. A great soft mass that toppled down from the clouds to deliver himself, his embrace, in wrath or affection. That's why they called him that: 'The Avalanche.' That's what they carved on his headstone. And that's what I was thinking when the broadcast was cut short...) The government called an election for November on the day I was to fly out, and when a few moments later I touched my chin I found a tear there, waiting; Marcello was dead. The news occurred to me like an old, buried memory, familiar yet inaccess-ible except through precise circumstance, a smell that rouses it from dormancy. Since finishing Marcello's autobiography, in my work as a kind of proof-reader I had been under virtually perman-ent contract by the incumbent government. I had overseen almost all of their significant public announcements and submissions. And yet I knew nothing significant about them or their plans, no knowledge that could be called upon autonomously. My work was rhetorical, a sort of intimate, literal engineering. Would that, by analogy, I had been working on a building (rather than, for example, a speech), I could not have determined its usefulness or aesthetic value, only assured you of its ability to stand and withstand. In other words I could speak only and absolutely of its (the building's, and nothing else's) integrity. So the government's announcements always felt to me like distant memories because in my work (and, perhaps, in all things) a sort of osmosis was inevitable. And because even the most highly-channelled mind is a relentless assembler of information, a stubborn maker of stories. For this reason I tried, in general, to avoid the television and radio. The news reel had become ghostly, and the nation's fate had begun to feel like something I had lived out (or lived *through*) before. I was in my car on the way to my mother's house when the news came through, to say goodbye. To her, yes, but also, finally, to my life as 'The Polisher,' a name that had penetrated or else inhabited me completely. A name that had brought me fame and fortune, each of which was modest and cruel. In other words, infamy and financial stability. Or else, again, loneliness and apathy. My phone was ringing as I rolled into my mother's driveway. I had not answered it for two days, afraid that at its other end my editor was waiting to cancel my assignment, a possibility I was no more willing to face than the fact that an election had been called. And that, within a matter of weeks, Marcello would not just be dead, but truly gone. The tired Queenslander where my mother lived, and in which I had grown up (with, and then without, a father) was too big for her now and she had students and migrants living in the rooms. The veranda was dry, raw and splintery, scattered with empty bottles and newspapers. Dead palm fronds leaned against the balustrades, brittle and bowed, hooked by their sheaths among and over towels and clothes. I had intended to go inside, but realised (and this, after five years, was a revelation) that I didn't need to, because just by imagining (and by holding my phone—which was ringing over and over now—fast to myself) I could move through that scene that never changed.

In the living room, the TV sat on the floor. The bowl of a stilted cot (once my own) was crushed like an egg and laid on its side against a wall, ragged cane at the fractures of its two broken legs. The couches didn't match and were torn, spilling foam. Indian and African rugs were pinned across windows and doorways, scattered across the floor and bunched in corners. There were no photos. A small table bore sagging candles and the table was fused to the floorboards by wax of many colours, generally blackened. The smell was foreign and putrid. Around a thin wall my mother sits (she, alone, is always in the present—not a memory but a fixture) in the kitchen at a laminated table with thin metal tube legs. She is hunched over some loose, printed pages. I wait, unannounced, at the doorway, and observe her in her ever-present. Her starchy, grey-black hair is tied up in a bun and the loose hairs make a kind of aureole that is lit up by the window behind her. She is a horror of obesity, balancing even as she sits, knees splayed, the shapeless dress of an Islander woman draped over her Danish flesh. Her feet, one bridge atop the other, and bare beneath the table; these are two strange, arced masses. Her ears, alone, are small and elegant. She raises her head first, and then her smudged pupils lift up to illustrate the small square glasses whose chain droops across her shoulders. It is impatience that always greets me, though I might have been missing, or standing right there, forever. My work until then may be described simply, or else in great and ultimately suggestive detail; I was indeed a proof-reader. But even within that specialisation I was a specialist, capable of living for hours, days, weeks or even months among the fine, structural details of a text without once concerning myself with its ultimate relevance or value or meaning. To be clear, I was not and am not an expert in the English language, insofar as I could not have put names to or explained in much detail the grammatical justifications for my work. And nor am I a gifted speller (though these days a computer can manage that). I simply moved from one word to the next, and occasionally back and forth within phrases, or sentences, or paragraphs, or else chapters or entire books, changing this or that word or punctuation or ordering of things, until I felt that a kind of equilibrium had been reached, or else (and this is only to best describe my experience) until I felt as though I could stretch out the whole text in one long line and hold it up to a light to be assured of its straightness, like a pool cue. I went by feel: that is as good as I can do to explain it. A finished text, to me, was a feeling of content or justice, like the end of an itch or an illness, or the trueness of a plane. I had studied to be a journalist, but as a student I had solicited my editorial gifts in an effort to secure the friendships that had always eluded me. As the demand for my services grew beyond the university campus, so did my solitude. In my usefulness I became repulsive. I soon learned that to be so specialised, so precious, and so highly in demand is to become the lowest form of life—an enzyme in the gut. I had always intended to return to journalism, to join my employers as peers, but the more important I became to them, the further I felt from being one of them. And it did not help my cause that those who engaged me were highly secretive about it (to the point of having me sign non-disclosure agreements), and that my reputation spread amongst certain connected worlds like a dangerous rumour. Politicians, noted academics, commentators and critics found their way to my tiny apartment, always by telephone or post. I became used to the idea of money in envelopes. In short, I was passed around the intellectual, political and cultural elite of Australia like a terrible secret. My explicit refusal to work with novelists and poets did nothing to deter their efforts to engage me. I am thinking of one in particular, who (though his face was covered by a handkerchief, so that I'll never be able to say for sure) having sent me numerous drafts in the mail, which I had dutifully returned, grabbed me by the sleeve one day and pulled me into a little grass area beside the train station near my building. Though he was quite old at the time, he was surprisingly much stronger than I was and had no trouble pinning me to a concrete embankment. His bald head and tired black eyes (eyes that were like looking down the tubes of old socks) were unmistakable, though I admit that neither of us took our hands away from our faces. He thrust a manila folder into my hand before swearing at me and running away. It was a collection of stories, some of them mythical, set in Brisbane, Launceston, and towns in Greece. I read them for pleasure, but ultimately returned them unmarked.

I still had not moved from my car (and the phone was once again ringing) when the front door of my mother's house came open and she rolled out onto the veranda like a fog (it was growing dark, and colours were fading), a ginger cat folded over her shoulder. If she saw me she did not show it. From down on the driveway, behind glass, she seemed tidal, gravitational; the scene warped about her centre. Her brow sagged, heavy as milk-laden sponges, and fell in droplets (she showered compulsively, prerequisite to moving from one place to another) onto the boards as she crossed them. Her hand rose and clung to the breach of the hammock, and she stepped, one foot before the other, up onto a small coffee table. With a profound shift of energy, she then rolled, shoulder-first, into the rainbow sack that swelled like a balloon to receive her, darkened, then started to drip. Before the car crash, my mother was a fragment; bony and stiff. That she survived, unscratched, was the first sign of her witchcraft. I was, at that moment, a ten-year-old boy nursing a box of triangular trophies for my father's rugby club. My father, uncontainable, toppled like his namesake through the windscreen and settled where gravity could keep him; they buried him on the playing grounds, among the laurels and jacarandas, so that it snows Brisbane purple on him in spring. They used to say that I looked like him before all the trophies rushed up out of the box with the stolen force of a head-on collision.

I ARRIVED AT ADELAIDE AIRPORT later that evening. A driver had been arranged to pick me up. The driver said that it was a shame we weren't travelling in the daytime. The way to the Gulf of St. Vincent was very beautiful. He told me I was going to have to imagine the farms and vineyards that would have started to appear a little way from the airport, as well as the ocean, which was out to the right of the road. We drove for an hour of long, gentle slopes and curves, undulations that felt natural and elegant. The darkness was compelling but not absolute. Occasionally long corrugations—two types of darkness—would appear out of my window, flashing by like a series of corridors or aisles in a library. My employer for this assignment was a small literary magazine from Brisbane that was paying me seventy-five dollars for my work. Needless to say, the money was insignificant. (I had sometimes charged over five hundred dollars for a single hour of "polishing" a text.) I was to conduct a series of interviews with Australia's most celebrated writer, who until then had worked under a pseudonym and never spoken publicly. The sense in which my involvement in Marcello's autobiography was responsible for this I had struggled to assess. And every time my phone rang I was increasingly convinced that, whatever the case, my involvement was now well-known, and that the editor was having second thoughts about my suitability for this assignment (upon one of two precisely opposed critiques that I knew were circulating: the first, that my work in producing Marcello's bestselling autobiography was sociopathic, that I had worn the sad old dying fairy over my writing hand like a puppet and made him my own horrific creation, that I might well have been some sort of deviant, a literary necrophiliac; the second, that I had simply demonstrated a weakness for men with personalities like gravity). I remembered then that the obtuse brief I'd received about this assignment included the instruction that I was not supposed to bring a telephone (nor a computer, which anyway I didn't use). I wound down my window slightly and pushed my phone out the crack, checking that the driver wasn't watching in the mirror. The driver pulled off to the left of the road just as we were about to approach a substantial hill, which gave me the impression that all the while we had been driving around the base of a giant bowl. The car bounced on the unlit dirt driveway, which took us through a group of trees that was brief but very dense. At the other side, we passed a tin shed and the driver pointed out some olive trees that surrounded the house itself. He left me at the doorstep with my two bags. Then he shook my hand and looked back down the slope in the land and breathed deeply, as if perhaps he had been there before. He said: This is going to look so beautiful in the morning. I saw the house only vaguely, but I knew that it was small and elevated on stilts. A woman (the author's wife, I assumed) came out to meet me through a sliding glass door. She said nothing. She was tired-looking, blinking in a slow and dispirited way. She wore a long dress, which sounded as stiff as military canvas, and one of those half-cardigans that cover only a woman's shoulders. Her eyes were very shallow, almost wooden-looking, and she held her right hand under her opposite armpit, as if it had been recently burned or cut. Seeing a row of shoes by the door, I sat on my case to remove my own. The author's wife turned away and revealed a small, ringless ear as she refastened a comb in the flank of her stiff, silvered hair. Her feet were bare and she had a black, floral tattoo on the bridge of one of them. Suddenly, I heard a scream coming from inside the house. The author's wife went to the door and I stumbled as I rushed up behind her. Her opened hand met my chest. She was staring through a small split between two curtains. Without turning back to me, she said please (as though to say, please, stay where you are). Her face was hard up to the glass and her head was turned aside, as if she was also straining to hear. I was so close that I could smell the skin of her neck, which was unadorned and slightly rancid. Inside, the voice of a boy was begging its father's apology. In turn, the father (the author, I assumed, and then shivered at realising that this was my first contact with him, by the distant sensation of his voice; it was as acute and thrilling as if he had crawled up and touched me in the darkness) was pleading for the boy to stop. He insisted that the boy was innocent. But the boy would not be denied the chance to admit to thoughts of which he was ashamed. This, at least, was what I could make of the exchange, punctuated as it was by the whispers of the father, and the intermittent delirium of the boy. After a while the boy began to choke on his pleas. I stood up on my toes to look past the author's wife. A bald, brawny figure stood with his back to the door, and then knelt out of sight. (I had seen him now, the author. I was perhaps the first to look at him and know who he was.) The boy's choking became coughing, and soon this too subsided; he insisted that his father order him, by threat, to confess. (Again, the father's replies were whispered, and I could tell only by tone that they were consolations.) The boy soon began to scream again until once more he was choking. His feet stomped on the floorboards, gradually with less conviction, like a wheel's final, unmotivated turn after its engine expires. He said a few more words, but what little sense survived in him was a dissolving thread. Then there was silence, and I returned to the seat where I had removed the first of my shoes. Concentrating on the task, and feigning disinterest in the drama that had ensued, I nonetheless heard steady, wide footsteps moving further into the house; I pictured the author carrying his exhausted son to bed, a thing as light and hopeless as a husk. While I was occupied, the author's wife went inside but did not invite me to follow her. For ten minutes I waited, looking from a cautious distance through the slither in the curtains behind the glass door. I heard the footsteps of two or maybe three people. Some light footsteps, surely of children. Once, I saw a dress brush past the opening. I heard whispers, but none seemed to answer another. Then all the footsteps gradually led away to somewhere deeper in the house. Eventually, the author's wife came out and brought me through the sliding doors into the now lightless room. She took my wrist and ushered me to another small room, where I was to sleep. The bed was small. There was an empty night table without a lamp and a desk without drawers. Above the head of the bed was a window that was too high up to look out of, even when standing on the bed. The roof was pointed like a chapel and its seam ran above the bed's centre. The window was open or broken and there was a looping sound of wind and shifting foliage and distant bird calls which seemed filtered and almost recorded. The walls were wooden and painted over with scattered white. After I had excitedly paced the small room a few times, I lay in bed, though I knew that I was a long way from sleeping and the dread of this possessed me mercilessly.

I BEGAN TO THINK ABOUT the election. The truth that I had tried so hard to ignore now had free reign over me; I could no longer effectively nullify my own vote by contriving to use Marcello's as its eraser. Marcello was dead. Marcello was dead. The last thing that Marcello had ever said to me was that his identity was "like a rabbit-hole through which I have only ever known myself to fall." He had said this into a Dictaphone that I later turned off when I returned from the bathroom to find him dead. I listened to those final words once his body had been taken away. But still I could not accept them. What is not understood is that by the time of his death Marcello spoke almost entirely in aphorisms of that kind. Aimless rhetoric such as: "The only wealth I have ever really known is the privilege of truth about myself." It is true that these words, indeed all of his words, he had made me promise to print. But insofar as he would have had me reduce his life to a philosophical treatise or a list of psychological self-diagnoses, I was obliged to deny him. My decision was to allow him to confess only to the truth, (I would not have him confessing to lies, or myths) and so the book begins with a rare moment of honest revelation, in a tone I had hoped to set and preserve: "At this time in my life there is little point any more in my hiding the fact that I am not Italian but rather Indian-Japanese. Take another look at a picture of me and you will see for the first time that this is entirely possible. With continued reading and eventual trust in what I reveal throughout this, my autobiography, the thought that my face has ever seemed Italian will be absurd to you. That no-one has ever thought to doubt this until now may seem to be a tribute to my instincts as an actor, but in fact that would not satisfy the depth of my performance. Many times throughout the years I have stood before a mirror, alone, and tried to remove this camp, Mediterranean façade that has become me. But on those occasions, as I consciously tempered all of the gestures and idiosyncrasies by which I know I am known, meticulously ceasing every contrivance of my demeanour, in order to be without my myriad qualities, each of which is both deceiving and deceptive, I am no more my true self than a little girl in her glittering slippers and plastic tiara is a princess. Yes, the name Marcello was given to me at my birth, but it has always been a pseudonym."

It would surprise no-one to hear that Marcello, in broken moments, could be eloquent. Eloquence, you could say, was his life. But increasingly his words, for all their charm, became a horrible self-satire. He was no more manipulative than he had ever been, but gone was the canniness which had made his lies an artform. I was forced to develop new criteria for identifying sincerity in his self-analysis. Now and then he would grace me with something that resembled truth, always without warning and when I was least prepared, so that I could not escape the thought that he knew all along what I wanted of him (but of course he did, of course he was playing until the last), though at the time I comforted myself by believing that in a moment of silent hysteria he had simply forgotten to be cruel. It was thus one morning, just as I was waking on the divan by his window where I sometimes slept, that he delivered, in these very words, the notorious and epic passage from the book's penultimate chapter: "My shrewdest commentators can surely now retire their theorising about my affinity, both creative and personal, with beings that have suffered a radical and irreversible schism in their image, specifically those that have been disfigured, whether in car crashes, industrial accidents, animal or human violence. You see, their grotesquery is a kind of permanent façade that they will always live in spite of—an irrevocable celebrity. My affinity with such persons is that we *are* our hideousness." Marcello had lain flat, facing the ceiling, just as I was now lying in the author's house. Or else he would turn onto his side, propped up on his elbow, his gaze always beyond me and beyond the walls. Sometimes over entire evenings he would talk unprompted and unbroken but for the coming and going of the nurse. I had always known that I was not the only one courting his confidence in order to write his auto-biography. In fact he had said from the outset that my love for him would only get in the way of him writing what he wished to write of himself. But I convinced him with my palpability and dedication, as well as by reassuring him that he would always possess the power to determine the final word, had he but lived to exercise it. (A promise that I surely cannot be accused of breaking, since the publication happened following his death.) After long evenings of dictation I would go back home in the morning and proof-read the articles for which I was well-paid. Still today my inner voice has Marcello's rasp and his lisp, and sometimes as I am working his robe will seem to appear in my eye's corner, or else I will seem to feel his fingers lightly brushing my head's left side, my numb side. I have long ago convinced myself of what others would surely refuse to grant me: that this is not the manifestation of my con-science for having betrayed either him or some ethic of writing or journalism, but that it is rather more innocently a kind of psycho-logical residue from those years of sitting and listening at Marcello's bedside. Surely I am at least entitled to take solace in the post-humous interest that Marcello is enjoying, an interest that had long abandoned him, even before we became close, some nine years ago, when (walking his dog along the Story Bridge on the morning of an election day, he'd seen my whitened fingertips clinging desperately back through the protective fence, as he would later describe, "like tiny white flags, signalling a precious soul in danger") he'd first had the novel idea to make us politically null for as long as we both lived. And made me laugh, with the exquisite timing of a friend or an imp. Just like that. Had I ultimately left him solely to speak for himself, I know for a fact that Marcello's star would never have shone again. He was no longer able to express himself other than through a sympathetic medium, and I was undoubtedly the last of those. With regards to the rare, apparently honest anecdotes and reflections that he did share with me: even these were so scrambled by qualification and so confused by contradictory accounts (in one story that emerged again and again over the course of a year, Marcello variously described the unfolding of a vicious schoolyard fight—once from his perspective as the victor, once as the brutalised loser, once as a sick child that watched from the window of his school's infirmary, and yet another time as though this story had only been told to him, by his father) as to be irreconcilable. Which is to say that in his own words Marcello did not even amount to a whole individual anymore. (To my critics, again, I ask if you know what you are saying when you call me a ghostwriter. Just as I ask those who so desperately need me, why is it so comforting to call me a mere "polisher"?) In the end, if Marcello's story was to be told, there was only me. Me and my willingness to make something out of the sinking illusion of his personality. I am not the first to describe him as a vortex, and yet I am the first to be accused of seeking to free him, for posterity's sake, from this self-consuming existence. (Not that others have been so kind, but I would like to believe that he would have wanted this for me too, after so many years of devotion—*absolute* devotion—during which, to the befuddlement of everyone who bothered to know any more about Marcello's life, I might best have been described as the keeper of his comfort. Only a week before he died, Marcello's nurse had watched us laughing to ourselves about something I cannot quite remember—which had become very rare indeed, our laughing together—while she changed his morphine. Under her breath as she left the room, rolling up the empty plastic sack, she had said that Marcello's pain was like a ghost, which caused Marcello to withdraw from his rare good humour. I knew at once that I would have the nurse replaced. Not that I had yet even considered the meaning of what she had said.)

Sometime that night, I left.

2

IN THE FOUR YEARS preceding his death, Errol Doyle was basically an invalid. He was, according to professional deduction, incapable of speech. He was likewise no longer capable of any physical movement, with the exception of the rotation of his eyeballs, very slow chewing, and manual gestures that were so subtle and incoherent as to have been deigned to be involuntary. Errol lived until two weeks after his eighty-second birthday.

On the night in question (that of Errol's passing), as was the New Year's Eve tradition, the guests were ushered across the foregrounds of the Lady Flinders Nursing Home to watch the fireworks display over the Torrens River. Those unable to walk were too many for the attending nurses to push in wheelchairs. Thus, the home's white Transporter was loaded with a handful of the lesser abled guests. Among those guests, in fact the very *least* able of all, and also the very last to board the Transporter, was Errol Doyle.

Errol's wheelchair and Errol were loaded through the van's rear by a device that raised them on two mechanical forks and then drew them backwards into the cabin. The nurses had decided to leave Errol in the van during the fireworks display. The van was backed up to the knoll at which all the other guests had been assembled, leaving Errol with a view to the river in the distance. As the last of the guests was helped out of the Transporter's sliding door and guided toward the huddle, Errol's fastenings were double-checked.

Once Errol was satisfactorily secured, the two nurses convened at the front of the van. The young male nurse leaned up against the bonnet, checked his watch, and impatiently watched a few seconds go by. The female nurse reached into the male nurse's pants and squeezed his genitals through his underwear. The male nurse flinched and restrained a burst of laughter.

The van's suspension, thus, shrugged.

The first explosion of the fireworks threw a plume of concentric red embers, followed immediately by a rolling series of crackling yellow ashes. The two nurses circumnavigated the van once more, checking that all guests were suitably distracted, (one travelling clockwise and the other anti-clockwise, both nurses peered briefly through the van's rear window at Errol), before moving away toward a small garden shed just out of view of the knoll.

Another of the guests in attendance that evening, one quite physically able by comparison with Errol, a solitary woman who spoke rarely, turned her back on the spectacle of the fireworks just as the nurses had disappeared from sight. The woman was taking advantage of the fireworks to illuminate the pages of a novel in which she had long been deeply engrossed. Her name was Ursula Flannery; having turned in the opposite direction to her fellow guests, she removed the small novel from a large pocket at the front of her nightgown, and raised it up into the multi-coloured light.

Curiously, Ursula only ever read while standing up. She had not read in any other posture, at least not since her admittance to the home. Furthermore, Ursula always moved as she read. In fact, in reading sessions that lasted a number of unbroken hours she travelled a considerable distance. And though she never took her eyes off the pages of her book, she rarely ran into obstacles. She typically moved along a clearance, a hallway, or relayed the width of a room. Ultimately, of course, the physical limitations of the house conflicted with the apparently limitless concentration of Ursula; she would soon find herself hard against a wall, a tall window or else a locked doorway. The only evidence that she was ever even aware of her location was the odd occasion on which she happened upon one such limitation and her book began to tilt towards her. Whereafter she would immediately turn and continue in the opposite direction.

The curiosity of all this is that, although she was definitely moving, Ursula was not actually walking. In fact, there were no discrete signs that she was propelling herself, nothing that could be determined with the naked eye.

On the first morning of 1990, in the coffee room of the hospital to which Errol Doyle's corpse was transported, the nursing home's resident doctor, who had attended to Mr. Doyle from time to time over the course of four years, was confronted or else amused by what he perceived to be something of a riddle in the patient's death. The riddle was either grammatical or else philosophical in nature, he could not be sure which, or if both in fact were true. Did the death of someone like Mr. Doyle, who was long devoid of all forms of expression, and whose only living gesture was to perpetuate his painfully subtle kind of existence, really seem to be rightly described as an "*event*"?

Subsequently, in a moment of literal mischievousness or else mere philosophical curiosity, the doctor considered drawing the face of an analogue clock with a thick, blunt hand, instead of declaring, digitally, the Time of Death on Errol Doyle's death certificate. Or else perhaps, he thought, he might enter the approximate dates and times between which Errol Doyle's death had occurred, dates that ought perhaps to have been years apart. He further amused himself by imagining a sort of axiom-based curve or else shaded graph that described Errol's death as a phase, the critical moment of which was a sort of technical abstraction that was near enough to incidental to the subject under analysis.

The previous night, at a party held in a mansion in North Adelaide, a woman had propositioned the doctor behind a brush fence in the courtyard. The woman had already lifted her dress to reveal the red and black laced knickers between her freckled thighs. The doctor, sitting on a wooden bench across the paved courtyard, cigarette in mouth, made it clear that he would not indulge the offer, generous and instinctively tempting though it was. "There, there," he said, "you've lost your head, darling. Too much champagne. I am flattered, of course, but think of my dear wife... I'll leave you now to get yourself together, and you'll soon be grateful that I've spared you regret." It was the third time in ten years that this kind of proposal had been made to the doctor. The three women who had propositioned him were the wives of his three closest friends. Indeed, this most recent incident completed a sort of trilogy of seduction.

At dinner parties, the like of which he had attended that evening, the doctor was quietly spoken and proffered very few opinions. Instead, he contributed the sort of rug-pulling Socratic questions that merely undermined the confidence of those who did invest themselves in their beliefs. The doctor felt that to do so was to slowly avail his own intelligence, or else his relative intelligence within his small and static social circle, by a process of attrition and elimination; while others were always guaranteed to be ultimately proven wrong, the doctor was *never* in a position of needing to admit to ignorance. Furthermore, in retaining an aloof position with regard to all matters of certainty, the doctor had delicately cultivated a lofty disinterest to the practical lives of those around him. He had adopted a way of looking across the table at these dinner parties without engaging anyone in particular, the way one species observes another. It was not an exaggeration to say that he saw himself as a kind of sage in their eyes.

The doctor tied his white hair in a ponytail. He kept a short beard and wore Hawaiian t-shirts exclusively, as well as sandals over socks. He was not an attractive man, and his two front teeth were false, fixed by a plate he removed when he readied himself for bed.

On the night of Errol Doyle's death, the two nurses sat—one on the lap of the other—on a small bench on the unseen side of the garden shed. There they had hurriedly shared two cigarettes and exchanged both oral and manual sex.

During the tryst, the male nurse had been listening carefully for the conclusion of the fireworks, an event that, he had briefly and annoyingly (as though, unconsciously) mused, was a sort of non-event, something that occurred because "nothing" started to happen, or else because a state of nothingness began. He was prone to those sorts of thoughts as a by-product of his education, whereupon rhetorical game-playing seemed to have become an unshakeable burden, like the need to masturbate.

However, before the fireworks came to a conclusion, the shrill screaming of Ursula Flannery caused the two nurses to return to the knoll, dressing frantically as they ran. The female nurse, affected by two hurried glasses of champagne and six painkillers, was both laughing and crying as she ran. Naturally, the male nurse perceived her hysteria as a threat, but was little able to subdue her while dealing with the issue at hand. It was not until hours later that the male nurse had realised that his belt was twisted in the loops of his pants, sometime after it had been noted that Errol Doyle had passed.

Consequent to the slight incline on which the van had been parked on that New Year's Eve, and also to gravity, Errol Doyle was leaning forward into the straps of the belt that fastened him to his wheelchair (that is, toward the rear window he was facing). This physical tendency could not be witnessed easily because Errol Doyle was a large and mostly shapeless man, the aperture of whose apparently upright posture was unusually wide. His head was lolling and his tongue was protruding from his lips. But this would not have alarmed anyone who'd been recently entrusted with his care. And yet the subtle forward angle into which he'd been positioned in the van made lifting the weight of his head, for the purposes of the circulation of blood and of breathing, just beyond the present capacity of Errol Doyle's feeble strength.

And so, with his eyes alone (which is to say, without even the control of his lids or brows), Errol attempted to alert the figure that appeared to be approaching the van's rear window of his terrible and likely mortal suffering. That figure was Ursula Flannery.

The immediate imperceptibility of Ursula's movement while she was reading might be likened to the hour hand on an analogue clock. One might say that the hour hand of a clock has a velocity that is, while definite, too subtle to perceive. Likewise with Ursula's movements. In order to see that she was indeed moving, one would have to look away from her for a while, and then look back again, noting the erstwhile displacement. In which sense, the invocation of a kind of necessary ignorance was the only way to recognise what was really going on with (or else happening to) Ursula.

On the night of Errol Doyle's death, as Ursula read her book and therefore moved toward the van (and subsequently toward the encapsulated and dying Errol Doyle), the light thrown by the fireworks bounced off the van's rear window, effectively doubling the illumination of the page she was reading. Indeed, would that one had no knowledge of Ursula's peculiar and inexplicable tendency to move while she was reading, one might suppose that her transportation toward the van's rear that night was the effect of a subconscious attraction to the light, for better or else clearer reading, like the slow turning of a heliotrope toward the sun.

The book that Ursula was reading was *Local Anaesthetic* by Günter Grass.

As soon as he was shown to the corpse, the doctor determined that Errol had suffocated. But the definitive role that this had played in his death was less obvious, so fine or else vague was the line between living and dead in the case of a man who, for so long, had described a sort of miraculous or else ridiculous parody of survival or humanity. (The doctor remembered how Errol had stared at him during examinations, the way a fish stares; that is, incommensurately.) Momentarily, thus, the designation of a Cause of Death seemed as ridiculous or else crude to the doctor as the Time of Death. It provided another titillating riddle for him to articulate; was it fair to attribute Errol's death wholly to suffocation, when, for all intents and purposes, the critical cause of his inability to sustain his own life was the fact that he couldn't support the weight of his own head?

Also, perhaps, obesity?

Despite these ruminations, however, Errol Doyle's death certificate was ultimately filed conventionally. (Cause of Death: Asphyxiation. Time of Death: 12:00 a.m.) For all his intellectual indulgence, and the artful manipulation of his social being, the doctor was ultimately a bureaucrat.

In truth, Errol's death was not discovered until the Transporter had been driven back to the home and an attempt was made to unload him. Even then, only after a long examination, many readings of his pulse, and more than twenty attempts to rouse his consciousness, were the nurses satisfied to declare that Errol had passed. Until that time, the focus of all resources, the cause of alarm and panic and the ultimate summonsing of the home's director from the party he'd been attending with friends (among them the home's resident doctor) was Ursula Flannery, who had broken into so violent an outburst that no-one—not even the doctor—could quite reconcile that frail old woman with the consistent testimonies as to her supernatural rage. (That the rear fender had been ripped off the back of the nursing home's Transporter by Ursula as she attempted to lift the van off the ground was a phenomenon so incompatible with common sense that it effectively went undocumented, and was relegated to gossip. This, despite the fact that the fender's repair was a matter of immediate business for the New Year.)

The director interviewed those of the guests in attendance on the knoll that night whom he felt were capable of reliable testimony. Some said Ursula rolled about on the ground, attempting to smother or be rid of something that had possessed her. Others, that she attacked the van in some sort of furious and vengeful fit. An undeniable bruise on her forehead was explained in three different ways (that she'd thrust her head at the van's rear window; that she'd repeatedly slapped her head in a fierce and ape-like gesture; and that she'd rolled around on the ground and struck herself in the face with a knee amid her self-entanglement).

The only common fact throughout each of these testimonies was that Ursula, during her outburst, had imagined herself to be on fire. But what had never been made clear to the director was *why* the analogy of immolation was so consistently put forward, given that Ms. Flannery had not, according to any testimony or medical report, actually been on fire. And nor did anyone attest to her having made a coherent explication from which her imaginary engulfment in flames might have been reasonably deduced. In the end, though, he satisfied himself with two (tenuous, if not creative) explanations. The first: that the simultaneously occurring fireworks display had associatively bled itself onto the subconsciousness of the guests that he'd interviewed. That in searching for an analogy they had clutched at that which was psychologically nearest: the fireworks under which all this had taken place. The director (like all supervisors of institutional homes) considered his work to be a form of practical psychology. One of his chief occupations, ever since he'd inadvertently witnessed his wife undress before the nursing home's doctor at a dinner party two years ago, was theorising a sufficiently compelling (while also sympathetic) analysis of his own state of mind in the event that he actually murdered someone.

The second potential explanation for the presence of fire in these testimonies was the director's own sense that some kind of danger and/or revelation might be imminent in his own life, that a spiritual channelling had taken place, that he was being warned or else tempted by something up ahead on the path of his fate. The director, deep down, was a spiritualist—a merely tenuous sign or "message from above" could compel him to do anything. If the clouds directed him to the edge of a cliff, he would certainly walk off it. He had never admitted to this extreme fear of ignoring or straying from fate, which he thought of as a narrow path lined intimately with razor blades.

Incidentally, one afternoon the following May, while driving away from a morning's examinations, the nursing home doctor's car caught fire, and was engulfed. The nurses at work inside the building ran to close the blinds and move the guests away from the windows, and it was then that Ursula's own death was noticed.

The director's report on the New Year's Eve incident imbued it with none of the theoretical, philosophical, or supernatural possibilities that its fulfilment had presented him. Relying ultimately on the consistent testimony of the two attending nurses, he wrote: Ms. Ursula Flannery suffered an unusual psychological schism manifesting in physical expression. A fit, or episode. Potential cause: unknown. Psychological analysis is considered.

Ursula Flannery's book had been confiscated on many occasions before the night of Errol Doyle's death. Each time, she woke in the morning to find the book missing from her bedside table. She had often spent two or three days recovering it, kneeling before each of the small libraries in the various wings of the house in search of the book's thin, bronze spine. Though the nurses had not explicitly conspired to steal and hide Ursula's book, they took a certain pleasure in observing the slow saga of its recovery. And so indeed, waking from drug-induced sedation and sleep the morning after Errol Doyle's death, Ursula found that her book was missing once again.

On the back of Ursula's book was a photo of the author. The photograph was black and white. The author (Mr. Grass) wore a furrowed brow and a stout moustache.

In the weeks following the incident, psychological examination (carried out by one of the home's young nurses in strict secrecy) revealed that Ursula had at some time in the past two years begun to confuse her own life's events with a number of those detailed in the book she'd been reading at the time. She had also come to believe herself an intimate acquaintance of the author. She had for many months sat the book on her bedside table overnight, the author's photograph turned to face her, in place of the portrait of her deceased husband that was stored in a case under her bed.

After a carefully plotted set-up (the young nurse, in her role as psychologist, left Ursula alone in her temporary office, and watched her through a jamb in the door) Ursula was observed reading another book, a book that had been specifically selected by the nurse for this purpose. This book was written by the same author (Günter Grass) in the same era, and was printed in the same bronze-spined edition as the book that had so conflated Ursula's memory. Indeed, it even had the very same photograph on the back cover. A book that would likely, for a few moments, be mistaken for Ursula's missing book, and thus cause her to pick it up from the table (which the nurse had set up to look like a psychologist's quarters). Incidentally, the replacement book was *Cat and Mouse*.

For the first hour, Ursula stared at the closed book on the table before her. She then reached over and turned it to face her, opened it in the middle, and stared at the pages. Yet another hour passed before she slid the proxy book into the large pocket in the front of her gown, left the nurse's office, turned up the hallway, and began to read.

It was so discovered that Ursula did not read in the conventional fashion of left to right, top to bottom. Instead, she merely opened a page and scanned, seemingly randomly, her eyes following no obvious pattern, and pausing only briefly between movements. Then, at intervals that seemed entirely random, she turned to another page, any page it seemed, and scanned in the same way.

"Considering her use of books to inform her delusion," the nurse theorised in her report, "one might reasonably view Ursula's manner of reading as being designed or of having evolved to service her psychological disingenuousness. She is looking for proof of her own life there, as a bee looks for flowers that resemble itself. Which is to say, not by visiting each flower on a single plant in a meticulous and ordered and exhaustive manner."

Lying in bed on the night of her second interview with Ursula (and oddly possessed by her dependence on analogy to accurately report on the patient's unusual behaviour), the young nurse likened her own personal experience of reading to the shuffling of a caterpillar, which first drags its back half up, then extends its front to advance. It had something to do with the burden of her mind, her cautiousness, and her desperation to comprehend everything around her before moving on. At the end of every page she had ever read, the young woman had glanced over to confirm the page number. Then she checked the number on the next page, to ensure that the one correctly followed the other. Like a caterpillar, she thought, which cannot move beyond or without itself.

The nursing home's director, having secretly employed the young nurse in the role of psychologist, accepted her analysis late one evening in his office. He had thought that according to the minor conspiracy in which he'd involved her, and to which she'd consented in full knowledge, it would be a matter of course that she would submit to a sexual advance. But once the nurse had submitted her report (charmingly, he thought, in a manila envelope), he realised that she was roughly the age of his daughter, and that anyway he hadn't the creativity to seduce a woman (even a vulnerable, indebted one) after thirty years of fidelity.

Once the young nurse left the office, he threw the folder in his fireplace, and invented his own brief report, which anyway he was certain no-one would ever read.

On the night of Ursula's outburst, after a few minutes of reading by the light of the fireworks (and of course, having moved in her mysteriously imperceptible and yet definite way), her book had begun to tilt toward her just as it had often done when she ran unknowingly into a wall or doorway inside the nursing home. She had looked up and seen that she had run into the rear window of the nursing home's van. The fireworks, as described, were vividly reflected in the glass. It was some moments before she released her focus behind the reflection and the glare and saw Errol becoming dead.

Early on the morning of New Year's Day, the male nurse who'd been supervising the fireworks excursion crossed the knoll on his way to the car park. There he found a book lying face-down on the lawn, between the damp pads left in the grass by the van's rear tyres. Miraculously, he recognised it as his own. He had taken the book into the house at a time that seemed so long ago now, the first year of his undergraduate literature degree. His notes were scattered inside. The nurse was in no way superstitious or inclined to believe in signs. But some kind of inexplicable clarity came over him at that moment. An aesthetic clarity, if you will. Not clarity itself but a *sense* of being clear, or else being capable of clarity. His thinking had broken through or else broken out of something. He, or else his thinking, was free (of something). He went home.

Until her death four months later, and for a while after, Ursula Flannery was referred to as 'The Witch' by a number of the female nurses at the home, particularly those of Mediterranean and Latin American descent. An interpretation of the events of New Year's Eve had become popularised among these women: Ursula, reading from a book that had since vanished into thin air, perhaps reciting a spell of some kind, and chanting it through the rear mirror of the van that night, had so nudged the delicately poised Errol Doyle off this mortal coil, so to speak. The nursing home's doctor might have been amused to hear that, in the opinion of the nurses at the home, the cause of Errol Doyle's death was not suffocation or obesity or negligence or even gravity, but simply and definitively: Ursula.

There were certain nurses who now even swore to having witnessed Ursula travelling through the hallways of the home. Moving, but not walking. They'd originally thought they were only seeing things, but it was obvious or else entertaining enough to them now to believe that she was possessed, a bad spirit.

This rumour (as is the nature of rumours, which have extraordinary gravity) was only fortified by the fact that Ursula, after a number of weeks spent searching, hopelessly, for her book around the home, had taken to sitting in one place every day, by the window but not looking out of it, without a book or a newspaper or anything, her hands crossed on her lap, and with a look on her face that was variously described as "arrogant" or else "satisfied" or "smug." Some of the nurses now crossed themselves as they passed.

3

I DON'T UNDERSTAND HOW we've ended up here. Though it's hard to explain what it is that I don't understand exactly. I really don't know what you want from me if you know what I mean. Or if you want anything in particular. Or anything at all. I mean I appreciate you bringing me the news. Though it's not good news. It's awful really. Appreciate is the wrong word I think. I knew Jimmy pretty well for a while there back when I was just starting out at my job. We used to hang out in our lunch breaks sometimes. Maybe once or twice a week. I mean I always knew he had some problems and I always felt for him. He's one of those guys that you kind of feel a bit close to because he never talked any shit. Or else I guess that's the reason. And when someone doesn't say much you kind of think that they just don't reckon there's all that much worth bothering about. And that kind of raises them up to somewhere different in a way. I'm not saying he was depressed for sure. I mean that's not the point is it anyway. Because the telegram says he was beheaded so. Jesus that really puts a lump in your throat saying that out loud. Hard to actually say. Excuse me. I mean the point is that he didn't kill himself obviously. That's the thing I'm saying. Not that you were asking about that. Anyhow look that's not where I was going, I just got sidetracked. Shit. Be*head*ed. What the fucking hell. What the goddamn fucking. What the hell's going on out there in the world. Or in people's minds. You just never really know do you. And Jimmy of all people. The guy was barely there. Not bothering anyone. Going about his shit. I once saw him just full-on crying on his way home from work. I mean I was driving my car and I pulled up at the lights and there he was in the car in the next lane just bawling his eyes out. And I mean *bawl*ing. Like the way kids cry you know. Like almost terrified or something. When I saw Jimmy he was just like that. In a real panic. His face as red as hell and so wet that he looked like he was melting or something. What do you do in that kind of moment. You know. When you see a guy who thinks he's alone just totally tearing himself to pieces like that. And especially when it's a guy of your own age or so. And a guy you work with too. Professionally. Me I just pretended not to see him and shot off as soon as the lights changed. Because you'd think the thing he wouldn't want is for me to see him like that. Something bad going on with him I guess and you usually just have to grind through it and there's no other dignified way. My ex-wife used to cry all the time in one of our spare bedrooms. Leaving the door just a bit ajar probably so that I'd know what was happening. And even though it's not the same thing for a woman to cry. I mean it's not as confronting or serious or something. Even so I knew that you don't go into a room when someone's in there having their way with themselves. Really it's something you should treat like masturbating. And I know that sounds funny at first but it's some- thing I overheard one time and have never forgot. And the more I think about it the truer it is. Really. When you stop to think. Any- way. Look the thing I'm trying to say is that I'm a little confused. And even though it's probably not a big deal I've got to start to put some words to my feelings here. I mean first of all I don't think I completely understand *who* you are. That's the thing. Like first I sort of thought you were just a messenger or something like that because of the coat I think. And the message. Wherever that is now. And really in a way that's still the only name I could give you if someone asked me now. Is *messenger*. I mean I didn't even know that telegrams existed still. I'd have said it was a wartime thing if someone had asked me before. Without thinking about it too much. I'd have said it was from a different time. I mean obviously it's not now I see. Here you are with a telegram if that's even what it was. I guess I've never seen one to know for sure. And now I've left it somewhere anyway. I'm just wondering then why you're walking around with just the one telegram or message and without anywhere else to go. Or so it seems. Because you've been here for so long now. I mean we're talking hours maybe. Is it. To be clear I realise that I invited you inside. No doubt about that. It was of my own accord and I wanted to. It seemed right in the circumstance. And at no point have I asked you to leave. I'm not saying otherwise to be absolutely crystal. And I know I kind of just started speaking my mind about all this stuff and maybe you felt like you had to listen. For a while out of courtesy. And surely you're tired now of me talking. At least of those ideas I was just talking about. Those three steps I'm looking into making into a bit of a program. Like a guidebook about people management. And how like I said it all relates back to my father and how he raised us. And actually I didn't mention but should have the way he used to sometimes throw his half-full dinner plate on the ground and leave the table and go and sit on his armchair on the other side of the room and watch my mother and sister and me in reverse. And how we knew that the thing was for us to be able to keep going and eating and talking among ourselves as though nothing had happened. As if he was still there at the head of the table. It was a bit of a game for my sister and me. Scary but still a game. And kids like that stuff. Though my Mum always struggled to keep her face straight and sometimes she went red and laughed and coughed because she was trying to stop it. And there were tears of effort and coughing or choking and occasionally she just got up and covered her face and ran off. And my Dad would follow her because she kind of lost the game and she knew it. You can probably see how that brings together what I've been saying about his way of seeing things. In case I wasn't making sense before and maybe now you'll get it.

Anyway it's all been a bit confronting this thing with Jimmy and I don't want to be ungrateful to you. It's nice for a guy like me who lives alone to have someone there when he finds out something like this. I mean I wasn't thinking this stuff consciously but you know in hindsight I guess that I was. Probably yes. I'm the better for being able to talk to someone. I feel like I've more or less told you my life story you know. I mean I'm not really the kind of guy that goes on like this with my childhood stuff and talking about the illness and all that. But you just sit there and listen and my mind's just racing in light of what's happened to Jimmy. I mean I'm really just a nine to five and relax on the weekend kind of guy you know. I don't reckon there's enough to say about me to fill a book or even a story or I didn't think so anyway. You just listen pretty *intensely* and that's the only way I can explain it. I feel obliged in a way except not obliged by you but by the situation we're in. And the fact that you aren't saying anything ever but still you haven't taken your eyes off me for hours. Not even to drink the coffee I made you. And not even with that thing where the little myna bird flew in through the veranda door and landed on the table and started pecking at the Monte Carlo from like right under your chin. And you didn't move or budge or blink or shoo it away and I was waiting for you to do something in response. Anything. But you just kept on looking at me and I just went on talking. Not knowing what else to do. And eventually the bird was gone and so was your biscuit. And with a combination of that and other little stuff that don't mean much by themselves the thing is that I kind of feel like somewhere along the line something that's a bit hard to explain has happened. And now somehow out of all of that and maybe just the passing of time I'm in a position that I don't want to say exactly *worries* me because the word seems wrong or else just unfair on you in light of your just kindly sitting by me for all this time. But definitely I do feel like I've kind of trapped my*self* if you know what I mean sir. It's not like you've been forceful or anything like that so don't get me wrong with what I'm saying. You haven't laid a hand on me of course. I'm definitely not suggesting there's been force of any kind. I mean it's hardly your doing this problem I've got now. So don't think I'm pointing the finger. I'm taking responsibility believe me. It's the *situation* that's got me concerned. It's just that I'm starting to think you know I'm starting to think it's kind of strange that we've moved from the kitchen into the outhouse even though I didn't notice feeling odd at the time. And in a way I don't really remember it all that well because I was talking about all that childhood stuff that takes a lot of concentrating to get out clearly once it starts flooding through your head you know. I mean with you sitting over in that dark corner so that I can't really make out your face anymore and still not talking or ever really even moving at all. And me just sitting here in the middle of the outhouse with the sun really kind of catching my face through the window so that it's almost hot in this spot you know. And I've got to kind of squint sometimes now. And in a really weird sort of way I kind of feel like I'm tied up with masking tape or rope or something even though you and I know I'm not. Just it's odd is all. And maybe you can see how it might be in hindsight. I mean part of me thinks with pretty good reason that the fact I'm feeling a bit funny is because I haven't had a drink since you turned up. And so look it's not the kind of thing I just go about saying to people but I think we're sort of at the point where I don't feel like it's much more of a thing for me to just admit that I'm an alcoholic. It's become important that you know and you wouldn't have guessed if I hadn't said because I'm not the kind of guy that slobbers or dribbles and I don't wake up in gutters or police stations or anything like that. I don't even go for the hard stuff you know and that's why you didn't see me reach for the bourbon when I got the news about Jimmy. No I'm just a guy that actually *needs* a little drink like on a regular basis. Like others need medication. And not much more than six or seven beers a day is just about enough for

me you know. Just one every two or three hours or I just get kind
of anxious more than anything. I start to feel like if I don't get a
drink soon I'll probably run up against some kind of not very nice
or just plain shitty thing that I've never actually run up against
before because I guess I've never had too much trouble getting a
drink when I need one. I mean when I say I'm an alcoholic I'm
being sort of technical. Not like characterising myself if you know
what I mean. It's not even a big enough thing that it affects my
work or anything. And like I said I've run a good little team in the
office for a few years now and Jimmy was one of them back then.
And we're known for hitting our targets and as far as I can tell
there's no kind of suggestion or whisper that I have a problem.
And I guess if you think about it I really and truly don't because
surely a problem has to cause problems you know. I mean it has to
be problem*atic* doesn't it. To count. As a problem I mean. At lunch-
time I'll head over to a sports bar in the mall just near the office
and have a burger and a beer or maybe two just like anyone might
do on a Friday you know. Except I'm doing it every day. And what's
the difference in the end. I mean it's no big deal for a guy to sit and
watch a game and have a beer with lunch is it. Because back before
I was moving up the ladder and making a real go of it and before
I was starting to see how maybe I had something to contribute and
not just to my own office Jimmy used to come along with me and
sometimes he'd have a beer too. And we never made any sort of
big deal of it or anything. Because you know as I keep saying which
maybe makes it seem like I don't really believe what I'm saying.
Even though I really do. And I can't see your face in the shadow
but I kind of trust that you're not doubting me or laughing or anything like that. And anyway the point is that if what I've got is really
a problem then it's low on the list of things that matter in the world
and it's even low on the list of things that matter in my world you
know. And really problem's not the word for it as I said. I'm only
telling you this because it's become necessary and I'm really hop-

ing that you'll be a little sympathetic and do me a favour now that you know. And it's funny because I was just thinking a little while ago when I was thinking about my management program that maybe the difference between people you fear and people you respect is as simple as them being either able or not able to be really and truly sympathetic. And maybe the difference is that sympathetic people understand your fears and show you with everything they do and don't do that they know what scares you. And with their own behaviour towards you they sketch the out-lines and shadows that make a really accurate sort of image of your fears that's like a photographic negative which is really maybe just a sketch or a picture of you. And you recognise this image of yourself in their behaviour toward you and that makes you feel both flattered and protected because it means they know you and know how to protect you just like they're doing by behaving in such a way that your fears are very clearly shown without you actually getting scared. And I was looking in the dictionary the other day for a way to make all that catchier and what I've come up with is that good managers precisely *e*voke but never *pro*voke your true and personal fears. And I think really that that's what respecting someone is. Whereas people you fear make you scared as though your fears were an inconvenience and that makes your own fears and maybe your actual *self* seem either irrational or irrelevant. To you. Which is not supposed to be related to what's happening here directly. I just got a run on again talking. I was just saying because I sort of feel as I said that I like can't move from this chair without your permission or something. Which is just so damn hard to explain since as I keep saying you haven't said a word and I'm in no way stuck to the seat or anything. There's just the odd sense in my gut that I have to stay put or else. Or else I don't know. I don't want to put a name to it. The thing is that right next to you there under that canvas sheet with all the dust on it there's an old bar fridge that I used to keep stocked here in the outhouse just in case. In case of something. Or maybe I just didn't have enough room in the other fridge at the time. I really don't remember now and I haven't thought about it for years. Because I mean I never usually come out here and well why would I. It's so dark for one thing. And hot. Anyhow the point is that there's bound to be a few old beers in there. Maybe Buds I'm guessing. So look then I'd like to come over there and pull the canvas back and open the fridge and grab myself a beer. And I know like you do that it's going to be years out of date and probably it'll taste like shit and it'll be stale and totally flat or whatever. But all that's really actually beside the point. Because I just need it now. And what I'm talking about is a *real* need and I'm serious about it. I might not look all that panicked but I'm on my way. And by that I mean of course that this whole thing is serious only as long as I don't get or feel like I *won't* get my hands on those beers. Because how can I put this. Getting the drink is the answer to this problem. And the problem is not the problem of me being an alcoholic. The problem is being an alcoholic and *not* being able to have a drink. And the distinction is so obvious to me that I guess it's like someone who needs oxygen being made to feel like some kind of degenerate or dependant. Because I mean you wouldn't call it a problem that someone has to breathe would you. No. But there are people out there who would. Trust me. My ex-wife was one of them. And I guess if one day she finds herself choking to death it'll be a kind of karma. But now so here's the distinction I'm talking about in my case. If someone gets his foot caught between some rocks while he's swimming underwater then that's a problem that both you and I and everyone including my ex-wife can recognise. And so it's a problem by the right name. And right now there's no problem here yet or else I don't think there is. And maybe that's because I'm like the swimmer I'm talking about. Only I can't tell for sure if my foot is caught under the rock or not. And maybe that's because all the sand is stirred up and I'm waiting for it to settle so that I can see if my flipper's caught or I'm just imagining it. So you see the problem really is a combination of or else a kind of *algorithm* if that's the term I'm looking for. No perhaps it's not. Anyway it's a combination of my being an alcoholic and you sitting right next to the beer fridge and looking in some ways or else to my imagination like some kind of security force or armed guard or something. Even though you aren't wearing any kind of uniform except for that tatty looking coat which I'm pretty sure hasn't got any kind of logo on it and I'm sure that you didn't know that that's where you were going to sit or what was under the canvas there or that I was an alcoholic or whatever. And of course you haven't opened your mouth to threaten me or tell me to stay seated or anything like that but here I am believing for some reason that I have to get your permission to get up and move. And that's where we are right now. I'm looking over or else getting a sense of what's over a horizon that's not too far off now. And there I can see myself being really and properly in trouble. And maybe now it's even true to say that I'm getting the first taste of a bit of the fear about the fear that I think I'm going to get about what I'm worried about. Tell you what. Okay. Let's both be aware that this is happening. That I'm making a decision just now. I'm just going to get up in one like smooth motion and take a couple of steps toward the fridge. I've got no choice in it really. As you can see. You have to believe me. I've just got to do it. I'm not able to sit down for another second in a very real way. So I'm just going to start to move. And it'll be toward you but not in any way *at* you. And I want you to know that. And I might just have to nudge your leg just a touch to get the door open. And when I do I'll just grab myself a couple or three beers and bring them right back to the chair with me. To nurse them. And that'll buy some time you know. That'll just sort of pull me away from the edge for a bit. So here I go. Again, I've got no choice in it. I'm getting up. Here I go.

4

A WHILE AGO I fell in with a group who called themselves mystics and were trying to run out of things to say. They lived by two rules in a small beachside town not far from where I lived at the time. The house was a small cottage that backed onto a river. The river had patches of reeds and mostly pelicans and gulls for traffic. The rules decreed no conversation and that nothing should be repeated. While I was staying with the mystics, I met a girl named Kathy with whom I walked in the mornings and afternoons along the red clay cliff and the beach. I first saw her following me. I stopped at the foot of the hill and stared back at her, but she would not approach. She leaned up against a tree, obscured. The next morning she was closer and unperturbed when I turned to acknowledge her. Two days later, she hooked onto my cuff with a fingertip. Having partially scaled the hillside, Kathy looked back down at the roof of the house (two of the mystics were gardening in the rear yard) and spoke; at that, my ambitions to empathise with the mystics, my sincere assumptions about their ideology, dispelled instantly. Kathy was unbeautiful, and passive in bed, neither forthcoming nor generous in foreplay. She, as with all the women mystics, was unshaven. Her hair was short and crudely cut and its felled lengths had been sold. I had initially noticed her at a meal; supine on a beanbag at the room's opposite side, legs carelessly splayed, revealing her bush to my neighbours and to me, oblivious or else liberal in the extreme. At every meal thereafter she fulfilled the same position and posture while the mystics affected their conspiracy.

From the room's edges and its few dispersed chairs, they shouted centripetally. Each of them offered a single sentence in turn. An order kept them from speaking over one another. (This was an imperative order, I realised in hindsight, because it prevented the happening of a disturbed and unfinished sentence, which would be unrepeatable according to the rules, and yet ineffectually banished. Suspended in the pure mental occupation of a paradox, this half-spoken phrase would have persisted timelessly.) I soon realised that Kathy and I had settled at the periphery of the rules and the order, separated categorically from the mystics and their task; we existed like stray animals sheltered in a monastery. Kathy's stomach and thighs were fatty and pale. Her nose was shameful, blunt and pierced. She was or else had been a filmmaker. She described herself as an artist, of a subcategory that called itself "conceptual." Her clumsy obtuseness was deliberate. Superstitiously, she never said the two words (conceptual, artist) together, frightened of their implications and spirit. Nor did she ever write them down in sequence, though she accepted them. She wore the qualification as a curse or a cross that was necessary to acknowledge if she wanted to resist it, like the illness of an alcoholic or a paedophile. In one of her films, a man walks through a park. His face is perpetually obscured by severe vantages, extremities of distance and angle, each of which is brief and unrepeated. The film is eleven minutes long, a ghost-story and an experiment in perspective (*"subjected* third-person," in her words). Kathy's left ankle bore a tattoo, her fore-hip also. A Chinese symbol and two crossing dolphins, respectively. The latter suffered unflattering contortions during monotonous and regular missionary sex. The mystics wore their contemplation utterly. During dinner their faces were serious and furrowed. My admiration for them was theoretical and relentless, my fear of them was condescending and impractical. (After watching them for a while in silence, I occasionally lapsed into a sudden and private panic at the sound of an elegant or useful sentence from one of their mouths, as though I was watching a small fortune of currency fall upon a fire. I reminded myself: for the mystics, the "currency" belonged to a country that was under absolute pillage, and was therefore among the only truly worthless things in the universe.) In Kathy's ignorance I saw myself as parody; her singular innocence violated the pious scene (I was possessed by the image of a child in pursuit of a loose dog during the solemn focus of a hymn). She ate greedily, sucking her fingers and occasionally snorting. When the blue dinner bowls were gathered, Kathy's alone sat belligerently on the floor. Occasionally I crawled across the room to collect it within my own. I awaited my banishment with the horrible certainty of a death sentence, conflicted in attachment to my aloof and sane position. Occasionally after dinner one or another of the mystics would remove their clothes and mount Kathy, pulling her dress up to her armpits, entering her dryly. I watched with premonition and jealousy; I was certainly more aroused at those times than when I slept with her. The other women mystics were also overwhelmed in this way, though it seemed less often. Kathy had joined the mystics after years of self-destructive and shameful behaviour. She'd never been asked to pay for food or board. Occasionally she joined a gleaning mission to the markets in the nearby mountain towns. Generally she stayed inside the house. She invariably wore a canvas dress and sometimes a duffel coat and military boots. When talking to me she held my hand, palm-up, in her own. She thumbed the bones searchingly. In my company, old emotions swelled in her. She dreamed occasionally of a party at which she was present but not in attendance. A moment of retributive heroism passes her by because of her omniscience; she is unable to pick up the gun or the fire poker, her hands drift across them like smoke. On the bench atop the cliff, her awkward fringe refused to obscure the sun; she always winced. Once, seminally, a philosophy student had made an art of her humiliation. He had ushered her, sarcastically, toward her psychological ruin. At one stage—preliminary, as it turned out—she spent some part of each day in the gymnasium showers on her university campus. The torrents of hot water dulled her self-flagellating and throaty screams. Later still, she assaulted her best friend and left her family home. She took a room in a lodging house. Four times in six months, she had her stomach pumped to remove vodka, wine, and cough medicine. At her lowest point she sat on a hospital bed and reasoned herself out of candidacy for an epiphany; she knew that her self-loathing was smarter than her. The mystics found her lying on Pottsville beach, drips and tubes taped all over her. (Incidentally, they found me in almost exactly the same place, though merely hungover.) Relationships inside the house were naturally unexplained. The privacy of an act determined its resonance; sex in the common areas was typically parasitic and inconsequential. Homosexual relations, apparently more sacred, certainly more passionate, took place exclusively inside bedrooms, though always with doors open or else ajar. When Kathy first met the philosophy student she had researched the topic of his thesis independently, remembering names and dates that she wrote down in a meticulous journal, in order to keep conversational pace with him and his friends. He was a number of years older than her, and her tutor. She understood virtually nothing of what she read, but she performed familiarity and insightfulness. In hindsight he'd surely been planning it all along; his compliments, his flattery, his encouragement, were the bait by which she was lured further into his rancid trap. Gradually, inevitably, and cynically, the focus of his study became more esoteric and confusing to her, the names and dates scarcer and less relevant. Historical fact gave way to conceptual puzzles and disingenuous language, which eluded her hitherto rote method of survival. She attempted to hold on. Night after night, sleeplessly, she tried to recognise the clue that allowed the philosophy student to pass off dispute or capture this growing and already incomprehensible riddle with his whole person, to instil in his subtlest movements—a nod, an ironic smirk, a knee folded—an absolute grasp of what seemed to her a bottomless pit of doubts. In a panic, she secretly deferred her law degree. She shut herself away from family and friends and tried to swim her way out of the murky intellectual depths into which, fraudulently and without licence, she'd submerged herself. On the evening that her own mother had shockingly and yet prophetically called her a slut, Kathy felt as though her soul was a placard hanging around her neck. She'd become unbearable to herself. She ran away. I told Kathy that I maintained a luxury boat owned by a Swedish man who took it out every two years or so. The boat was moored a few towns to the south. I was also a professional tournament fisherman. I had written and self-published a book of fictional essays about rare fish collectors called *The Deserving Cloth*. I'd been homeless for most of the 1990s, and was truly ill, mentally. Kathy said that her brain didn't let her *understand* anything the way most people's did. It only let her remember: things and processes, like a computer. Occasionally, when she was ruining herself for the philosophy student, dredging through essays and commentaries of essays (which, she said, were never related in the lock-and-key way that she hoped), she felt as though she was pulling at a door and also pulling at the other side of the same door. She never knew if this was an indication that she should stop, that she was foolishly wasting energy on a reflection, or whether instead it was a kind of test, and that she should continue to pull, and that ultimately she'd overcome the weight at the other side, which was not really her own reflection but rather some worthy obstruction, nearly but not quite equal to her potential self. A kind of present out of which she could emerge, in the future, better. And perhaps all understanding took the perfect disguise of one's immediate and ultimately surmountable self. The mystics occasionally went to work on local farms. They were mostly paid in produce and old clothing. When the house was empty I looked through everyone's belongings, piled up in cupboards or in the corners of rooms. Most of the mystics had valid licences and some had bundles of money. I found two suicide notes, a lock of bloody hair (fresh), a stuffed mouse, a pair of glass eyes, a box of bullets, and a small gun. All of these items were hidden in socks tied off at one end, identically so. At other times, reading one or another impenetrable essay, Kathy occasionally caught onto what seemed to her to be a critical notion, and felt as though she was beginning to open a box that contained everything she was struggling to understand; she ripped the wrapping away and tore it open. Inside, at once unfortunate and yet hopeful, was another box. This next box, since it fit within the first, brought her closer to the centre, to understanding. And so she seemed then only more certainly to possess, in her very own hands, necessarily, the answer to all of her questions. She opened it, and found yet another box. And then another, and another. And so on until she accepted, beyond the very strictures of reason, that the boxes were not getting any smaller. The town had one main street and a number of caravan parks. Walking alone one afternoon, I became lost, and woke in a trailer with a woman asleep on the other side of the cabin. Her tracksuit was blue and came off without her waking. Fights in the house never crossed the sexes, occurring only between women, inexplicably, or else between men when homosexual encounters devolved. They tumbled naked out of rooms, bloody and enraged. My interest in the fights was instinctual, though I grew bored of them. Kathy had made another film about lovers or conspirators who flood a small apartment. Watched through glass from beyond the small apartment's balcony, the couple escape, leaving the flood to rise and ultimately spill down the building's side (the camera was suspended in midair a few metres beyond the edge of the balcony, said Kathy). While the vision remains on the flooding apartment, the sound follows the couple. They drive to another location that might be a hotel room for the night, or an underground bunker in which they are gassing themselves; they discuss the nature of robot warfare in depth, and then Communism, before ultimately and seamlessly falling asleep or else losing consciousness. Comprising a single, one hundred minute shot, the film ends with the sudden destruction of the camera by a marginal character, credited, last in order of appearance, as "Impatient Audience Member." The mystics were not immune to corruption; whispers were inevitable and briefly comforting. A broken and distant conversation, separated from me by a thin wall, involved Kathy and an abortion. The tone was easily mistakable, but seemed humorous. Kathy was gone for the next two nights. In secrecy I read the thriller wedged beside her mattress, walking alone again to the cliff. I carried her up the hill on the morning she returned. She hung limply in my arms, shameless in entitlement. A sudden heave of rain coincided with my announcement that I was a misogynist, and also, conspiratorially, camouflaged my tears. I left not long after that, by which time Kathy was recovered and the fact that she had had an abortion at all was in perfect doubt. That morning one of the older men in the house had come into a room where I was lying down and crawled onto my back. He ripped my shorts with his ropy, hairless, grey arms. My head was facing the door and his arm was pinning it to the floor. A crowd amassed at the doorway or so it seemed to me between the fronds of my now long hair. The old man put his mouth hard against my ear. His breathy whispers echoed and reverberated and sent a wave of shivers down me that his three fingers, jagged and thin, rode into my anus. I protested in good faith, scratched him at the hip. There seemed to be a fight at the doorway, a fight to be witness, but none would enter. Except for Kathy, in her sacred obliviousness. She crawled in unnoticed between legs, moved docilely toward me on her hands and knees, turned and retreated without breaking rhythm. She soon settled in her own atmosphere, curled up against the wall. Her eyes batted sleepily, generally, in my direction. I fought some more, respectfully, and bit a cheek, then let myself be held, in silence, as the man's old body wound down, slowly eased its vigour, and dripped off me like a wet shell.

POSTSCRIPT: Years later, I fell unreasonably, and took myself to hospital. Cancer, of an aggressive and advanced kind, was found in my brain. My eldest son (brutish, and part-Aboriginal, thanks to his mother) brought a change of clothes to the hospital in a canvas bag, inside of which I recognised long forgotten artefacts from my time with the mystics, including Kathy's thriller. I found a number inside the thriller's cover and asked my son to drive me up to Brisbane. For two days, without telling him anything, we searched for Kathy, and eventually found her. She was thinner, certainly, and working in a legal firm. Her boyfriend, with whom she seemed eager but not familiar, was tall and effeminate, evidently a doctor. One morning I broke into Kathy's small apartment overlooking Southbank and found a wooden machine of sorts. The machine had two pieces, roughly the shape of a human, which appeared to come together to mould a body. I contemplated the mechanics carefully, and discovered that by small handles and wingnuts it allowed the pressure of the mould to be increased *from within*. To the effect, exclusively, of compressing the person contained. The machine was obscenely clean and its pieces raw; the smell of freshly sanded wood filled the apartment. On Kathy's computer I eventually found the files that contained her films, and watched them in sequence. Some of the files were corrupted. The next night I intercepted Kathy on a bridge on her way home from work. She recognised me at once, and ran her fingers down my face pitifully. It was hot, but she wore leather gloves with tight cuffs. After some drinks she drove us across the city in a hatchback and parked out the front of a two-story building with long, white vertical bars running around its entire façade. The building was lit by two powerful streetlamps, the metal bars virtually aglow. She explained that it was the location of her last and unfinished film. A revenge film, she said, or else revenge as a film. I remembered then how some of the films I'd watched the night before were shot inside. I had seen, from reverse, the shadows of these long metal bars on the faces of actors within, in strange, short clips that seemed to have been discarded ends, senseless, like something extra-textual or subsidiary, from behind the scenes. (It had occurred to me at the time that only in a digital age did such things survive out of passiveness, existing as they did without occupying space.) We were staying in a hostel nearby. Kathy dropped my son there and walked me to an unlit park. She pulled her dress over her head, leaving her gloves on. What I thought was underwear turned out to be a very tight strap that fastened a small, solid, thick leather pad over her vagina. She lay face-down on the grass, and then arched her back slowly, shifting her knees forward until they sat almost beside her ears. I was presented with her tightly knotted anus, lightly strewn with a rash, which seemed to be an uncanny and sympathetic reading of my fear of progeny. Kathy's hands appeared between her legs like insects emerging from the corollas of flowers. Intimately lit, they proceeded to pick and tear at her flesh-coloured stockings.

5

MY BROTHER AND I stood on the sidewalk outside the iron gates of
Doña Isabella's complex. Her bare feet hung over the rail of her
second-floor apartment. A streetlamp hunched over us and made
a blunt, heart-like shadow of us on the pavement. Doña Isabella's
feet were white and almost as if see-through. We could see the
little gusts of cigarette smoke sifting over the railing and over her
feet and then up into the night sky. I called out to her and then
her feet disappeared and then her face appeared. The old woman
looked down at us and the lenses of her big, clear-framed glasses
glared violently. Doña Isabella put her finger to her lips and then
she went inside and came back and threw our key out onto the
street and made the gesture for us to be quiet again. When I opened
the door she was there blocking the doorway and she grabbed
me in her little arms and called me her precious boy, *precioso*.
She was pot-bellied and had no tits and through her nightgown
I could feel a hard seam of tissue that ran across and down her
somehow like a crooked sash. She stood back and looked at me
for a while and then she glanced at my brother Gabriel across the
room. She walked over to her ash-tray and looked in it. One of her
legs was limp or slow and when she moved she swivelled her hips
to drag it along. Her cheeks were soft and loose and covered with
patches of meshy veins. She had a tiny forehead and a bulging
crown that was nearly bald at the top. Her arms were cold and
felt raw like mince. The long, pearly chain of her glasses hung
down to her waist and her glasses swung under the bulge of her

potbelly. I asked her how she'd been and she rocked uneasily back onto her heels and she rolled her eyes and said she had died waiting for us, she always died waiting for friends, and then she stroked my cheek with the back of her hand and I smelt her skin which was sour and soapy. Gabriel unfastened his backpack and dropped it on the floor and Doña Isabella threw a scolding look back at him and put her fingers to her mouth again for him to keep quiet. I have another guest in this moment, she said, *un artista,* he is exhausted, he has gone to bed, tomorrow he is going early to our poor neighbourhoods, he wants to see them, he has a privileged life, so he is curious, she said. The little Peruvian woman that lived with Doña Isabella came out from the kitchen and waved at us. She waved without moving her wrist, winking her palm. She had a darkly tanned face and twisted, thin black hair and she was short in the same way that Doña Isabella was short. Squat or squashed. I said to Doña Isabella that we'd talk to her in the morning and then she kissed my hands and turned to Gabriel and drew a cross and she said, the lord blesses your dreams.

When we got into our room Gabriel took off his clothes and sat on the end of the bed and talked inaudibly under a cupped hand into his mobile phone. One of his legs was crossed over the other. He was biting his nails and spitting the husks at the opened window and when he'd finished with the phone he took out his earrings and put them in the pocket of his toiletries bag. Then he went to the bathroom to shave his head. I knelt under the window and unpacked my pyjamas and then I changed into them. Out the window the airport terminal's backlit yellow sign was glowing on the glossy bitumen and the street looked soft and wet. There were two taxis on the side of the road at the airport's main entrance and the drivers leaned back against the doors of one of them and they were listening to music from the radio. A palm frond was nodding against the window sill and I reached out and steadied it and when I did I could feel that the air outside was denser than the air inside and felt like smoke. The fans at the end of the beds were on high and made a cutting sound.

Before sunrise the next day our alarms rang and Gabriel and I got up quietly and made our beds. The walls of the room were a dull, yolky white and the plaster was slightly rippled like a cave's inside. The shadows of the ripples leaned away from the bedside lamp and made the wall look warped. Between the windows and over the heads of the beds were photographs of Doña Isabella's daughter in her communion dress. She was albino. In the photo the lace of her dress stretched across her pink shoulders and up her long neck like a web and her hair was cut sharply over her eyes like a doll. She was holding a little umbrella that had the same white lace as her dress and her face was flat like she was pressed against glass and she was cross-eyed or not looking straight. We made a pack with towels and sunscreen and a change of underwear and went down to the street and to the beach. There were a few cars on the avenue and most of the restaurants were closed and there was a young woman standing in the chemist's all-night booth and she was reading in the light of her cylinder of glass. There was a line-up of food carts chained to a fence on the corner and a man was sleeping under them between the wheels. Some taxis slowed down as they passed us and flashed their lights rapidly. The avenue then turned to face the Old Town in the distance and the old buildings behind the blunt wall looked pale and papery. We took a narrow path between some houses toward the water and the ground was full of rocks and shells and a white, chalky dust that floated up-wards. Our sandals crunched over the shells. There was dog shit and horse shit and dead fronds that had fallen and some empty beer bottles here and there. The end of the path put us onto the beach and we could see the Old Town in the distance again. The haze had lifted and it looked like a photograph from a magazine with the sun shining in behind the wall and the buildings looking shadowless. Gabriel took off his shirt and his grey sweatpants and he stretched his arms out and faced the sun that was rising. His stark white skin looked malleable like putty caked over his bones. The sun was dulled by a film of clouds on the horizon and it looked like a torch was shining through a bedsheet or a shirt. Gabriel's shoulder tattoo was a rose and an eye weeping and his back was pale and strewn with moles. There were some black kids sitting on some rocks that came up out of the water a little way off the shore. Gabriel pulled up his bathers and fastened the drawstring. The water looked like soft metal. The sand broke and shifted in chunks and was cold and moist under the crust. Gabriel watched the kids on the rocks as he stretched his skinny legs against a hollow log that I pushed the bag of clothes into after I had changed. I followed Gabriel into the water and we swam. The water was the temperature of the air and the air was dense and the water seemed like only a thickness. I put on my snorkelling mask and started to follow Gabriel in laps along the shoreline in water up to my waist. I stood sometimes to take a breath or to clear my mask. I watched Gabriel go close by me underwater like a shark with his eyes looking ahead and his bald head dragging little bubbles beside it like gills and his bathers which were pale like his skin. After a while I stood up and looked around and he had swum out alone to the rocks where the little black boys were sitting. He talked for a while from the water spitting jets at them and then he climbed out and stood in front of them dripping and one of them touched his tattoos and he let them and showed his muscles. I got out of the water and waited and after a while I called out to him and he dived back in and swam back. We had breakfast at a little *tienda* near Doña Isabella's apartment. The young man at the counter remembered us and he cooked us scrambled eggs with tomato and spring onion and made juice from mangoes that he picked off a display beside our table. The sun blared around us instantly and I squinted. A dark toothless man parked his tricycle under the awning's edge beside our table and went inside and then came out again. He was silver-haired and his jeans looked new but the knees were split. The man swept his brow with a finger and his sweat clung like gel. His singlet said Cartagena and the letters of the word were rippled like the sun's reflection on the sea and they were multi-coloured and fluorescent. His tricycle had a plastic-shaded carriage and next to him there was another tricycle that was pulling a trailer of avocadoes. The driver of the second tricycle was younger and solid and he was leaning up on the handlebars with his eyes closed and he was maybe asleep.

When we returned to the apartment Doña Isabella was in the kitchen and she came out in a long floral nightdress that fell to her ankles and her large briefs showed through the material like a diaper. I could see the shadow of her nipple or a legion or mark of sorts around the middle of her chest. She asked us to sit and her croaky voice kind of echoed and she grunted and wiped her mouth and her hand shook and she clamped it between her legs and coughed again softly. The Peruvian woman brought Doña Isabella a mug of coffee and sugared it before her. She whispered something to Doña Isabella and then started folding laundry on the glass dining table behind us. I asked about Doña Isabella's youngest son. He lived in Miami with a girl from Medellin. Doña Isabella waved her hand in the air and the Peruvian woman brought over a photo of the couple. Doña Isabella's other son, Jose-Alberto, was a priest. He had attended a seminary in Santa Marta. The photo of him on the mantle looked ancient and the paper was yellowed and moth-bitten. His horn-rimmed glasses were large and his nose was big and Jewish-looking and his hair was shiny and had deep grooves and sat flat across his brow. In the photograph Jose-Alberto looked past the stare of the camera that had taken him as if something behind the camera was odd or concerning. Doña Isabella said that he had come home, recently, to Cartagena. He was living in quarters in the commercial part of the city and he'd begun to speak to the congregation at the *Iglesia Maria Auxiliadora*. I said that I was glad that Doña Isabella would be able to be close to her son again and

she said that Jose-Alberto was the very Lord's blessing and then she
patted my knee. The old woman picked a small cross out of her
dress through the neck hole and kissed it. Then she clasped my ear
with her cold hand and held it for a while.

Gabriel and I went back to bed and I woke soon after. I thought
I had heard strange noises in the other guest room or the next apartment and I went to the bathroom to shave my head and shower,
and then went back to bed. I woke again at midday. Gabriel was
sitting on the floor massaging his testicles with his back against the
foot of his bed and he was wearing only a t-shirt. His heels were
tucked up against his buttocks and his other hand was splayed on
the floor beside him and his eyes were closed. The thin skin rippled
finely across his pink, hairless stomach like a skinny cat cleaning
itself.

We went back down to the avenue and Gabriel wore a ribbed
singlet under an open white shirt with short sleeves. A big gothic
logo surrounded by flames stretched diagonally across his shoulder-
blades. His shorts were knee-length and denim and they hung low
and sagged off one hip and his knees and ankles were knotty and
hairy and the block-lettered waistband of his black underwear
showed when his shirt flapped up behind him in the wind. He had
leather-looking sandals with gold buckles and a pin-striped fedora
with a soiled and worn point and one of his ankles had a small
chain around it like both of his wrists did. We bought *empanadas*
from a cart on the footpath. The kerb was all crumbled. At the traffic
lights ahead two young girls stepped in front of the cars and juggled
and we stood by the cart and spooned salsa into the mince and
drank Cokes. Someone black was calling out to us and we were
ignoring him. The man with the same avocado trailer that we'd seen
in the morning turned around the corner that we were standing on.
He swayed heavily from side to side and groaned as he pedalled
like he was pushing through sludge. His wide back swept in and out
of the striped shade over his head and the bright white material

of his shirt was flashing like a broken light. We got in a taxi that took us past the Old Town to the *Boca Grande* and on our way we passed through the shadow of the Old Town's wall and glimpsed through an opening the horses and carriages and their drivers eating lunch in a huddle and blocking our view right in. We got out at the nearest end of the beach and walked as far as the blue kiosk where we sat at the bar on a half-log bench with our feet in the sand. The barman recognised us and we ordered beers. The barman bent his whole body over the rim of a massive plastic drum and he grunted as he reached to the bottom and made the distant sound of icy water shuffling. His bare, black arm trembled and glimmered with beads of water as far up as his bicep. The beers chimed like solid glass or metal bars between the knuckles of his one hand as he opened them and gave them to us. They were nearly frozen. We turned away two lady masseurs that came toward us smiling with buckets and dripping sponges and tried to convince us to hire them. After a second beer the barman pressed us to buy the lunch and we told him we'd think about it and soon after we accepted. We ate whole fishes and rice and plantains out of Styrofoam containers that a young boy delivered to us out in a metal shopping trolley with big rubber tyres. We moved to a tent just on the edge of the minor cove that had two splintery deckchairs covered with mats and was looked after by a tall, dark man with an opened shirt and knotted chest hair and bright sandshoes and a bucket-hat. The man scrambled awkwardly with his long legs across the beach between the tents, kicking up sand behind him when we or someone else waved at him. As he waited to be called for he sat at a picnic table by the roadside where two men were playing cards and laughing. The beach was full and people were lying in rows under rows of shades or sitting at the kiosks and drinking.

That's them, said Gabriel, and he turned about in his chair and looked back at the blue kiosk. Gabriel was squinting and holding one knee up in his arms. The *negritas*, he said. I walked over to the kiosk and I put my hand on the bar next to the two girls that were standing there and they greeted me in Spanish and then in English. I gave the barman some money and directed the girls across the sand where Gabriel was sitting and he turned around in his chair and looked back at us and waved. The girls held onto each other's shoulders and took off their high heels and they waved back at Gabriel once they'd taken them off. Gabriel stared at them as they moved across the sand towards him and he stopped waving. I followed the girls closely and held my palms against the smalls of their backs and they giggled and whispered to each other. *Dios mio*, said the shorter of the girls, *gemelos*. She turned back to look at me again and her teeth were large and wet and she asked if we were twins. It seems that we are, said Gabriel. He got up from his chair and kissed the girls each on the cheek and he offered them the chairs we'd been sitting in. They smiled and giggled and accepted but kept standing. Gabriel introduced himself and then me and I stood with my hands behind my back and the girls' shoes hanging off my fingers. The girls were dressed in tight tops and pants that clung to their bodies. Their makeup was purple and looked solid and Gabriel asked them if they were sisters too or else friends and they smiled and said that they were old friends and they played with each others' hands and fingers. Gabriel kissed the girls again and the shorter of the girls grabbed onto his arm when he touched her cheek. The girls rolled up their pants and sat in the chairs and I waved to the man looking after the tent and ordered beers and Gabriel told them to talk to him. The shorter girl was called Maria-Lady. She had a large, pronounced forehead and under it her face was small and she had tight balls of flesh on the points of her cheek bones. Her breasts were big and ripe-looking and she was solid and her bulging ass and thighs pulled her belt-loops away from her belt. The hairs down her jaw were dark and sharp and the wrinkles in her cleavage were thin and pale and like the skin on custard. The taller girl was called Maria-Elizabeth and she had a thin, pretty face and her eyes were small in large sockets and her temples were re-cessed and her cheeks were hard and flat and her hair was braided stiff. She had a tiny, hipless torso and she lifted her shirt to sun it in the chair and her stomach was hard and muscular and her naval protruded palely, like a thumb forced through a buttonhole or a small, grey mushroom. Gabriel stroked Maria-Lady's arm and told her to get undressed and that he wanted to see her out in the water. She took his hands and kissed them and she apologised and said that they hadn't brought their bikinis and didn't realise he'd wanted them to. I reached over and held Maria-Elizabeth's earrings. They were large, beaded hoops with hanging feathers and I told her they reminded me of dreamcatchers and Maria-Elizabeth thanked me and blinked and looked away shyly at Gabriel who was squatting down so that the sun bisected him and his legs were splayed about Maria-Lady's chair. Gabriel told them that he'd asked for them to bring bikinis today specifically and that he'd been clear about it and was promised they would. Maria-Lady rubbed his thigh and tilted her head and she hung her lip sulkily and said she was sorry and didn't know, really. She shook her head and ran her finger up Gabriel's neck and behind his ear and then she rubbed his earrings and then ran her long fingernails over the studs. *Pappi,* these are pretty, she said. She asked Gabriel if he thought that the earrings would look nice on her and I watched her other hand playing with a gold crucifix that was resting on her big tits. Gabriel grabbed her hand firmly and furrowed his brow. He lowered and shook his head and said that it wasn't her fault, and he rubbed the top of her terse thigh with his palm, and he called her beautiful and kissed her hand. It's not your fault, he said. And then he said it again and took his hand off her thigh and combed through the sand coarsely. Maria-Lady reached down and lifted his chin with her finger and asked him if he liked her body and if he thought that Maria-Elizabeth was pretty. Gabriel shook his head and smiled and was groaning softly. No doubt, no doubt about that, Gabriel said. He put his hand on Maria-Lady's thigh, sliding it toward her. This isn't your fault, he said again. His other hand was almost buried in the sand. Maria-Lady snatched it up and pressed it to her throat, and she breathed deeply in silence. Then she pushed him away and stood up and she pulled her yellow top over her head and threw it in the sand. Her breasts sat up in her blue-lace bra, fatty and trembling, and the pale, serrated stretch marks across her lower back were thick and deep, and her hands were on her hips. Her thumbnails were painted intricately. She held her breath and stretched taller and she looked like something inflating. I swim like this, *Pappi,* she said. For you I swim in this, she said. She fumbled with the button of her pants. I patted Maria-Elizabeth's head and she looked up at me and smiled briefly. Gabriel stood up and grabbed Maria-Lady and her flesh looked warm and rubbery and she laughed and resisted and squealed. Gabriel lifted her off the ground and her laughter was loud and sharp like a series of claps and her gaping mouth was a shock of big, spaced teeth and raw flesh and moisture. The ashes of swirling, glazed pink and brown and white looked like something melting. Gabriel put her down and picked her shirt off the sand and handed it back to her and said that he took her point and then grabbed her again and put his face in her armpit. I took Maria-Elizabeth for a walk along the beach and I showed her the scar on my nape where I'd been stabbed and she ran her finger around the thin lips of hardened tissue and I felt like she was pressing a coin or an amulet into me. Maria-Elizabeth had tiny, bony shoulders and hairy forearms and she was not noticeably paler in her palms or her armpits than elsewhere. When I asked her to show her tongue it was long and slender and ruby-pink and kinked at the tip and some of her mouth's inside was grey-tinged. Her perfume was flowery and sweet and strong across her throat and I saw her wave to some-one as we walked but when we stopped I told her to tell me who it was and she denied it. She pulled my fingers out of her mouth and stroked my hand until I softened my grip and then she put my hand on her fleshless backside. We paused under the shade of a lifeguard's tower and I pushed the hair back off her brow with the heel of my palm and she played with my belt. I smelt under her hairline something like herbs and meat. We went back to the tent and Maria-Lady was sitting in Gabriel's lap and he looked across at me behind her shoulder and smiled and then he told the girls to meet us tomorrow at eight, outside the Old Town, under the Café del Mar, and they thanked him and left together holding hands and carrying their shoes. We drank more beers under the tent and the plastic gradually sagged over us and came closer to our heads. Gabriel fell asleep. I watched the stream of merchants pass with inflatable toys dragged in giant nets and painted shell bracelets and ice creams and beer and photos of the island called *Playa Blanca* and I began to drift in and out of sleep. I woke once with cold water on my feet. A large woman squatted like a Sumo wrestler around my foot and rolls of sagging flesh hung between her knees and she clung to me tightly until I convinced her to go away. She got up and put her sponge in her bucket and left and was smiling and I put on more sunscreen and was squinting and felt that my cheeks were burning.

We rode the airport bus back to Doña Isabella's apartment while the sun was setting. Gabriel leaned his bald head against the window and I watched him from the seat behind and across the aisle. His mouth was slightly open and showed his little teeth. His eyes were narrow-slitted and his head was flat and his jaw shallow and wide like a snake. He smiled occasionally like he was thinking of something and his lips drew back at the corners as though pulled from behind him by hooks. He licked his lips from one side to the other. The bandaid on his neck was horizontal and bisected a yellow and purple shadow of bruising. When he licked his lips the sound was the sound of paper on paper. His lips were dry and grey before and after he licked them.

We got off the bus at the intersection by the *tienda* and Gabriel started walking and I followed. The houses in the area were all like villas and they had wrought-iron fences and long balustrades and they were all two-storied and brick. The trees stretched out and met over the street. There was a white wall of tall hotels and apartment complexes on the waterfront and we walked between two hotels. I could hear the ocean and when we emerged at the edge of the sand we turned and walked back without stopping. Gabriel walked ahead and I could see that there was someone else further ahead and that we were following him. Gabriel's head glistened under the lamps on the corners. The backs of his ears were thin and glowed red and seemed almost transparent under the street lights. Around a corner I saw that Gabriel had stopped altogether and that his hand was pressed to his ear like his ear was bleeding or else he was listening to his phone. He waved at me and then he started to run across the fronts of the villas and then turned beside a hotel and headed toward the water. What I remember most about this dream was that I felt lopsided as I chased him, like I was numb on one side, or else like the hotel I last saw him turn around had its own gravity or inertia that was pulling at me as I ran beside it. And also that when I reached the water's edge I was alone and there was a small, empty building hidden in front of the hotel that might have been a kiosk or a restaurant that hung out over the water. The windows were smashed and I couldn't see anything through them and the water was echoing loudly inside.

Gabriel woke me when we reached our stop. We ate dinner at the *tienda* and he told me that he'd seen the other guest on the bus, the one that was staying with us at Doña Isabella's. The guest had got on just near the castle and then he'd got off at the same stop as us, and Gabriel had watched him walk down the road to Doña Isabella's when we went to the *tienda*. He was young, said Gabriel, maybe in his late twenties. And Gabriel had been watching him on the bus, looking over his shoulder, and he'd seen him drawing something indistinct in a sketch book. Gabriel said that it was a very strange drawing and the young man's hand did not seem very agile or fluent, and Gabriel didn't see his face.

The next morning Doña Isabella's son was sitting in the living room when Gabriel and I returned from lunch and a swim and he greeted us in English and shook our hands with both of his hands. He invited us to sit. Doña Isabella was out buying *tamales* and Jose-Alberto offered to go down to the street and find her if we wanted to join them for lunch. I apologised and I explained that we had just eaten and were due to meet friends. You have many friends in Cartagena, said Jose-Alberto. He was wearing his clerical collar and the shoulders of his black shirt were sharp and his arms seemed fastened to his ribs. I mentioned that Jose-Alberto had lost more weight and he stood and patted his stomach and then he rolled up his sleeve and flexed his bicep; I keep fit, he said. I am sure to keep very fit these days, he said. The soul is in the muscles too, he said. Jose-Alberto offered us the tray of biscuits and *boca-dillos*. He played with the rings on his fingers. The rings were big and crude and soft-looking though his fingers were thin and bony and with tufts of wiry black hair on the knuckles. The Peruvian woman came in the front door and walked to the kitchen without looking at Jose-Alberto or at us. She went to the door of the other guest room and knocked on it a few times and then opened the door slightly and slid a plastic bag around the door jamb and closed the door again. She went to the bedroom that she shared with Doña Isabella and she closed the door behind her. Jose-Alberto was looking at us and we were looking at him and he asked if we had met the other lodger. I shook my head and Jose-Alberto looked out the glass doors beside him and smiled slowly. He shook his head and a gleam slid around the frames of his chunky, black glasses like something flying past a window. The jewel in his main ring was the yellow of honey. He has befriended her, said Jose-Alberto. My mother, Doña Isabella, he is sketching her, he said. I asked who he was talking about. The lodger, he said. The other guest who has been here for the past week, he said. Jose-Alberto's chin was oily and freshly shaved and he ran his opened hand up his throat and then massaged his lips with the tips of his fingers and his hand was like a bug crawling. Jose-Alberto said that he didn't know as much about art as he would like and that that was not the vocation he'd put his time into. A man is a body of hopes and ambitions and possibilities as diverse and as wide and as profound as the ocean, yet life is but a narrow passage through which only so much water can pass, he said. His eyes went from me to my brother and then back to me and he gestured with one cupped hand over his lap, rolling his wrist faintly, as though shuffling marbles or dice. I glanced at Gabriel who was looking at Jose-Alberto. But I have not seen these drawings, said Jose-Alberto, as they depict my mother naked and they are not for her son to see. He got up off his chair and walked over to the glass doors and stood in the sun facing away. His black shoes were shiny and big-soled and they looked at once like military boots and children's school shoes. I glanced at Gabriel again. I have not been to Australia, said Jose-Alberto. It is one place I will for sure make a point of visiting. Europe does not interest me very much, it is old, like my country. Have you been there, to Europe, he said. I shook my head and Jose-Alberto turned his head back toward us. His feet were still facing the window and he swivelled his shoulders around and then he said something that he didn't finish before Doña Isabella came in the door. She carried a steaming plastic bag and some other bags. Her hair was tightly combed back and a few strands fell over her brow and a sack of loose skin hung out of her armpit like a turkey's neck and was pinched and strangled red. She greeted us breathlessly and her cheeks were flushed and her wrinkled lips looked dry and her face was washed in a mustardy colour. She fluttered her dress and sighed. Jose-Alberto approached her and she took his head in her hands and kissed it to her sternum. Gabriel and I stood and excused ourselves.

At night we stood on the side of the road with the Old Town wall right behind us. The spotlights from the ground threw our shadows back at the wall and the shape was big and blunted by other lights. A large military truck approached slowly on the road from the South that ran between us and the water and the truck was pulling something. A crowd from the café that hung out over the wall of the Old Town gathered over our heads and the people were pointing at the camouflaged truck. The music throbbed distantly behind the crowd and the fluorescent lights strobed around the shape of them. Behind the truck was a jet or the shape of a jet wrapped in brown canvas and ropes like a present and it looked like a giant toy or else a giant moth. The truck approached and passed slowly like a ship and the crowd grew and some people began to cheer and then the whole crowd joined in. When the truck had passed the crowd disappeared again. A big man on a bicycle with a trailer attached appeared across the road and stopped directly opposite us. The girls arrived in a small blue coupé with darkened windows and Maria-Lady got out first and then helped Maria-Elizabeth out. They came toward us without looking back at the driver. They were wearing the same clothes as the day before except Maria-Lady's hair had a yellow flower in it. Maria-Elizabeth carried a purse and her hair was out and she had a thin, gold chain around her waist and her eyes were strewn with sparkles.

We walked around the outside of the Old Town and went to a bar under an old block of apartments and we sat outside and could see the Old Town over the road. The bar was empty and a man came out and served us and Maria-Lady asked for the bathroom and went to it. The floor was concrete painted red. Maria-Elizabeth sat next to me and she wrapped her leg around mine and laughed and surged forward and her head hovered over my lap. The knots and ribs of her skeleton were fragile and the hairs on her lower back were black and radiated like palm-leaves. She picked up my hand and kissed it and then held it. Her palms were loose-skinned. The man serving our drinks sent out his wife to bring us food from a restaurant and we ate a plate of *empanadas*. We ordered a half-bottle of white rum and the girls mixed the rum with an apple-flavoured soft drink. The woman that had got us the food watched us from inside the window and was also reading a magazine. Gabriel and I had a shot of the rum. His eyes were red when he looked at me to say cheers.

Maria-Elizabeth's eyelids were stretched tightly. They sat off her eyes at the corners like awnings. The void was big enough for a cotton bud to fit into and pull back so that a finger could force its way under her eyelid. I traced her spine through her shirt and she dragged her fingers up into the backs of my knees and her nails were smooth like teaspoons under a cloth. Gabriel and Maria-Lady walked off down the street and when they returned she was laughing and slapping at his hand and he was holding her buttock. He whispered into her ear and bit her lobe and she squealed. Her fleshy arms swelled between the grip of his fingers. Gabriel and I were wearing our cream-coloured pleated pants and burgundy button-up shirts and he was wearing his fedora and a scarf and his rings and chains. Gabriel went off to the bathroom and then afterwards he snuck up and crouched down behind Maria-Lady's chair to surprise her. Maria-Lady's teeth were large like thumbs and her eyes rolled back to show their pink-threaded whites. Her breasts were paler than her face. Her nipples were big and hard and they jutted out through the ribbing of her top. Gabriel leered up behind her and fell across her shoulder and bit her on the breast. Maria-Elizabeth laughed and slapped my legs and stomped her feet on the floor. A white plaque or scum was building along the flanks of her tongue and in her gums and tiny bunches of bubbled spittle were sitting on her molars. I went to the bathroom and when I returned they were standing and Maria-Elizabeth took my hand and locked her fingers between my fingers and we all left. While we were walking she said that my brother was nice but that I was the nicest one, the sweetest one, her baby, her beautiful baby, so cute, *tan lindo*. Maria-Elizabeth had a slightly husky voice. She ran her fingers over my cheek and clicked her tongue and pinched my chin and said, *mi bebito, mi bebito,* my baby. She massaged my hands with her knuckles and when she swallowed, her nostrils contracted. We walked toward the Havana Café in the next street and when we got there we ordered strawberry mojitos and sat down at a table inside by the front. The four of us danced and the crowd was full of dark faces and it moved to the loud music altogether and felt like the ocean surging. The band was large and the music was full of rattling wood and tinny horns. Gabriel took Maria-Lady outside. Maria-Elizabeth and I sat at the little round table by the barred windows. A crippled, ash-grey hand came in through the broken window and I first ignored it then gave it a coin. Maria-Elizabeth covered her little breasts and looked at me. Out of the corner of my eye I watched her fingers tap on her upper arms like Morse code for someone across the room. I got up and told her not to move and went to the bathroom and when I returned Maria-Elizabeth was not there. I stood on the chair and looked around and saw her balancing against the edge of the crowd near the stage. She was looking up at the black and white photos of Cuban musicians on the walls. Her arms were tightly folded like she was cold and someone danced into her and she fell sideways but kept her feet like a wave had hit her but not knocked her over and when she recovered the crowd had wrapped itself around her and she disappeared and then reappeared near a window. She moved along the wall with the crowd against her back, edging closer to the door. She squinted harshly like something was in her eyes and I went over to the exit and intercepted her and grabbed her by the arm and pulled her back to the table. I found Gabriel and gave him some money and on our way out Maria-Elizabeth grabbed Maria-Lady and hugged her. They stood in the doorway and looked down at their mobile phones together while I opened a taxi door and looked back. Their faces were yellow-lit by the screens and I called out to Maria-Elizabeth and then I yelled. Maria-Elizabeth got into a taxi and then she kissed me and looked at me and stroked her fingers across my head and then she grabbed my chin again and called me *bebito, el bebito, mi bebito,* my baby. I stared ahead and she lowered her eyes and dropped my hand and turned away to look out the window and started to cry then stopped and then laughed a little. The taxi climbed the hill to the west and I looked back. The ocean appeared behind the buildings and the tips of the buildings jutted out over the Old Town wall and the highest was the point of the church in the middle.

The next day Gabriel and I rose early and we packed our bags and made the beds neatly and we left the key on Doña Isabella's table. We went to the *tienda* and ate breakfast and the owner of the *tienda* told us to go to the quieter beaches to the north if we hadn't been before. He walked us to the avenue and hailed a taxi and told the driver where to take us. We drove past the airport and over a bridge and turned off the road at a red radio tower like the owner of the *tienda* had said. A group of young black men ran beside the taxi bidding for our attention. They offered boat rides and also tents and food. We negotiated a price on a tent and lunch and settled on a stretch of sand and we were alone for almost a hundred metres in either direction. I rolled joints and we smoked them and then I went for a swim and the water felt silky and thick. A man walked toward us with a long tray of fresh fish and we chose the ones we wanted to eat and the man gouged marks into their heads with his knife and then he walked back up toward the road. We ate and then I fell asleep on a square of sarong. I opened my eyes and the sky was bright and cloudless and looked frosted over. Gabriel paced the water's edge with his hand against his ear talking on his mobile phone. He was smiling. I used our backpack as a pillow and my phone's alarm vibrated quietly deep inside. A black man walked down the beach toward Gabriel. The man was thin and neatly muscular and he was wearing tiny blue shorts and sandals that he stopped to remove. He tied a thin piece of line to his leg and baited a hook with something in his hand and then he walked past Gabriel and into the water. Gabriel was walking up the beach with his back to the man and talking into his phone. The man swam out past the little waves and laid on his back and then only his head and his feet were visible. He raised his hand and tossed the bait in front of him and the line stretched and flickered in the air and the bait made a small splash and he squirted jets of water from his mouth.

6

GOOD MORNING. Or is it afternoon? I wasn't expecting you. Not in this moment. Not this exact one. Though I know I should always be ready. It's strange, though, that you should turn up now. I was just having some kind of bodily outbreak, sitting there on the toilet. In fact I was crying. Not from sadness but from a physical malfunction or else outbreak, as I said. A gland must have given way or spasmed perhaps. First I thought the roof was leaking, maybe the bathroom upstairs had flooded or a pipe somewhere was damaged. You know at this age my eyes are mostly all a blur anyway. So I didn't notice them filling up with tears. It wasn't until I touched my face that I realised. Needless to say, the book I was reading in there is destroyed. Completely. You'd think I dropped it in the bath. The pages have soddened together. I don't even remember what it was now. The floor is flooded too. If you turned around you could see it bleeding into the carpet from under the door. I never even knew I carried so much in reserve. Water, that is. It's incredible to think I had so much to lose. You'd think that I'd be thirsty. That explains my pants, too, if you're about to ask. I'm an old man but thankfully I haven't wet myself yet. Though if certain faculties of the body can just go into freefall like that, who's to say it won't happen eventually? It seems at times like I'm becoming a child again, ambivalent to self-control, a passenger to my own physiology. It's not the first time something like this has happened to me. Just the other day, as I was sitting in this chair, I heard a knock at the door. A woman I had never seen before came in and told me that she was my neighbour. From a few stories up. She asked if everything was all right. I closed my book in confusion, dragged my eyeglasses down my nose so that I could see her better, and said yes, of course. Then she told me that I had been screaming for fifteen minutes. So I took my glasses all the way off and started to clean them on the sleeve of my robe. Me? Was she sure? She said my voice was unmistakable, and that this was not the first time she'd heard me screaming, but that it was the first time she'd decided to come down and stop it, because on that day she was hosting a wake. It was true—she was wearing all black and lace and she looked like she took her mourning seriously. The dress, however, did not seem to fit her. She was awkwardly folded into it. Her skin was all bunched up around her throat, sagging over the neckline like a bit of soft coral or a sad flower. In any case, she was unmistakably sincere in her state of mourning, by which I mean that she was perfectly expressionless. Her face was plastered the sheerest shade of white. For a moment I suspected, or else fantasised, I can't honestly tell you which, so let's say I imagined, that she was not at all a person, but rather an inanimate object, a big piece of plasticine that had been dressed in a gown and painted to resemble a middle-aged lady. Then she breathed and her breath was like ash. I told her I didn't realise, and she turned and then moved away quickly, like she had been freed from a sticky web, or trap. I'm sure that I frightened her. Not that I moved a muscle toward her. Not that I looked at her lecherously or threateningly. There's no good in my asking myself what it is about me that is frightening. I'm just old. Too old. And I guess you always run a certain risk when you let yourself into a centenarian's apartment. You've a good chance of finding something terrible—death, or else some sign of its imminence. Or perhaps a pair of soiled pants stuck hopelessly to a pair of knobby old legs. Or an expression of irreparable resignation, a look that says, yes, every one of your faculties is an illusion, right down to your bladder control. That which is learned can be lost.

Of course, *you* know this better than anyone. Not only that every man is a temple of vanities, but that this apartment has contained some terrible things. You've seen the worst. I know for one that you found me and unhooked me from the ceiling the time that I hanged myself all those years ago. That's right, I've finally remembered. About three weeks ago now, I stood up on this chair to change the one lightbulb in here, the one hanging there right above you. As I was standing there something happened to me that seemed at first like *déjà vu*. I saw myself in the very same spot, reaching up to the ceiling, only not to change the lightbulb, but to tie myself up to the hook above your head there. From that little seam of *déjà vu*, which was like the tip of a snake's tail, or a section of its glimmering scales amid tall grass, a whole memory then slithered out toward me; it was thirty years ago, I was enveloped by real sadness, I jumped off the table, the ceiling didn't creak and I remember wondering as I hung there why it hadn't creaked. I also remember excruciating pain. Then nothing. So now I know it was you. Only you could be so cruel. My world has long been intolerably small. But before that day, or else before I accidentally unsettled a memory of that day, just a few weeks ago, a memory which ultimately lunged at me with its jaws gaping, as though its territory had been threatened, this room was the exact image of my claustrophobia, tiny and encroaching and excruciating, yet fair. But now that I have remembered what you did that night, the world I occupy has shrunk to resemble a coffin, or else a shoebox, or else the eye of a needle, depending on whether for your mind an image must be plausible in order to be terrible. So now that you know that I know, I want you to know also that I haven't opened your package. Mind while I just reach under your chair and retrieve what you came for, though not as you have long expected to find it. There it is. Brown paper and jute string. The bane, and sadly also the centre, of my world. Pick it up and turn it over if you like. Here, I'll do it for you. Check every angle and corner. There are no tears in the paper. The string is still fastened by that impossible knot of yours. It has never been opened. Inside, we both know, is a black notebook. Or perhaps I shouldn't be so quick as to presume. Perhaps, on this the five- or six- or maybe seven-hundredth occasion, what is inside is not actually a notebook. Common sense begs me to doubt it, though. Two weeks ago I hid it under that chair so that I would not look at it and be tempted to open it, out of habit or else fear, which are the same thing in this case. Every day, every hour, I looked at the chair and wondered what you would do when you saw that I had not so much as tugged at the ends of the string. I suppose I will get my answer sooner or later, the moment of truth is certainly upon us. Hold on, if you will, it has just turned cold. Did you notice that? Thank God for Sister Luz, the well-endowed angel from Mexico City, for this poncho, which she left behind some years ago now. Though it's a little small, a little emasculating in colour, I would surely freeze without it. I don't know if her prayers or her blessings could ever be as eloquent as this poncho is warm. It's as good as a miracle. Wait one moment while I bring the milk in from the window ledge. It's never the same once it's been frozen. I know I've said it before, but it's true. You cannot reverse the effects. All substances have memories. All are scarred. None forget. The milk is no different than anyone or anything. I think it was you that once wrote that the weather is like a mood. I remember your turns of phrase from the very beginning, Agent Vell. Sometimes whole passages return to wake me at night. I believe that every word you ever wrote back then is deferred somewhere inside of me, awaiting a moment to secrete on my consciousness. I know that it satisfies you to hear that. Though sadly, or else thankfully, on the other hand, I retain nothing of what you write these days. Sixty years ago I wanted your words to be a world. I tried to raise your every sentence from the page, to lift it up and turn it over, like some improbable invention or else a strange animal, to see the force or mechanism that animated it. Under your roughness of style

and your crudeness of ideal lay an immense philosophy, such as
cannot be rediscovered at my age, but which I glimpsed from behind
the tears of someone lost or else banished forever. How is it that
I once felt so impossibly old in your eyes, whereas now, at one
hundred years of age, I have become your infinite junior? I seem
to have learned again to foster a child's naivety. Today I do all in my
power to read your words without understanding them. I open
the pages of your notebooks only slightly, feeding my eye-line in
like a needle, starving the words of too much light. And then I scan
those words furiously, as though my eyes were being chased down
and over the pages, by an insect or an assassin, frightened and
faltering and confused. I go on reading in one horrible rush, until
everything is returned to its pile of infinite darkness, until I can
close the cover forever, which is really to bury your words once
again in the centre of the earth. You would think it the easier thing
to remain ignorant, but it takes all of my energy to read with so
much ambition and so little imagination. It is as hard a thing to
do as receive a knife in one's stomach without breaking the skin.
A pound-of-flesh-like conundrum. Your notebooks have become
an abyss into whose depths I must glance, quickly and wincingly,
craning forward but leaning back on my heels, aware of a kind of
gravity that wants to pull me in. Hold my hand for a moment, would
you? That's it. Just while I sit myself down again. I've learned that
if I squeeze something in my fist then the pain in my back tends
to hold off a little. Still, the pain is enough that I would scream if
there was any use in it. Strangely I don't remember ever wondering
what the value of my discomfort was until now. I really do think
that I've reached some kind of threshold of late. For a number of
years now I have been flooded with sensations from my childhood,
melancholic and sweet, my mother's voice before I knew her name,
my father's bitter armpits. The sights and smells are so vivid that
they amount to more than memories. They are more like summ-
onses. I have always maintained the image of a lifetime as a circle,

or else a loop, the completion of which is to approach the beginning again. Recognising what has already passed, one dies. Out of duty or necessity, I don't know. It is simply the way that things should happen. So I think to myself as I recall my childhood that this must be it. I have come back to the beginning, take me now. Nothing, alas! Nothing but nothing. Just the marginal fact of remaining, and of knowing that you will deliver your notebooks and return to collect them at the month's end. I still cannot help but wonder how old you really are, Agent Vell. Two hundred? A thousand years? I know you can't answer. That's what that look of condescension on your face means. Condescension sinks your eyes to another league of emptiness. If only I could forget that there was a time that your visits here were a pleasure, perhaps the single undisputed joy that my wife and I shared in forty or so years of suffering together in this tiny apartment. In hindsight it was an era, a phase, a passing demeanour. Back then we knew you simply as Pierre, and we received you like a blessing. I can still see the terrible stitching in wrong-coloured thread across the shoulders and elbows of your travelling coat. My wife learned to sew just so that she could make those repairs. She was always eager to prepare you food out of what precious little we had. It didn't bother her that you never thanked her, nor ever ate a mouthful of what was served to you, that you wouldn't even budge to make it easier for her to mend your coat. None of that ever defeated her affection for you. It was something quite different that caused her ultimately to forget you, and to return to her sad and dogged task, to remain unmoved on her knees throughout your visits. You lived too long, Agent Vell. She worked it out in her own way, by a woman's intuition, a woman's impossibly hidden cynicism. That's the truth of it. Wait a moment while I put the milk back out on the ledge. It seems to have warmed up a little again. The only thing less tolerable than defrosted milk is milk which has gone warm for a while. I'll leave the poncho on for now though. It brings me a kind of comfort, the thick wool and its dull weave. It really belongs to my wife, though she was never alive to receive it. Sister Luz or else one of her followers left it behind after their prayers some years back now, folded nicely and tied with a ribbon. I guess you'd call it an offering, a gesture, left for my wife for who knows what purpose. Appreciation or maybe sympathy. I don't really know how religion works or what it aims at. But it has always seemed like the right thing to do, to take the offerings made to her and hide them away, or else put them to use somehow. As a child I used to put out milk and carrots for Santa Claus' reindeer. Someone was always sure to take it away before the next day. That seemed to preserve my faith. I have a small box of things under the table. Perfumes, napkins, sunglasses, scarves, and lots of rings, lots of jewellery in fact, and some tiny leather gloves, none of which I can do anything with. At least I could make some use of this poncho, small though it is. Mind one moment while I use your shoulder to brace myself and sit down again. I'll just squeeze you there. I suppose all this back and forth is spared in apartments with refrigerators. The hourly migrating of milk and other perishables when the weather can't decide what it's doing. Can you imagine a refrigerator in here? Where would it go? It would look like a building inside a room. A man of your size can touch all the walls of this place without getting off his chair. While for two people, learning to share the space is something of a terrible and dangerous dance. One lapse in concentration while walking to and fro and a nose is likely to get broken. I can't imagine another apartment on earth that is so small. And yet for a few elusive slips of paper, this miniscule apartment has proved bigger than the whole of France. Many decades ago, Agent Vell, I sat in this very chair, shivering and chattering and soaking with sweat. My heart felt like a handful of hot glue, or else maybe wax, slipping by my organs on the way to my feet. I won the deeds to three apartments that sit side by side atop a hotel in Rome, with a view down the Spanish Steps, out to the Vatican, and beyond.

And then I lost them, hours later, without leaving the chair. Quite a feat it must have been. My wife had loathed Paris since almost the day we moved here. At first I was convinced that I liked it, but I came to feel the weight of this sad, secretive town, this petri dish for a culture of melancholy. The way they suffer here, willingly so, causing trouble when trouble is hard to find, makes you think the whole city owes a mystical penance. Take this poncho, for instance. Why has Paris not adopted this garment as its own? The atmosphere here is famously fragmented. The city itself is a kaleidoscope of microclimates. Have you ever descended from the November streets into the Metro? The rapid change in humidity is enough to make one light-headed. And yet they wrap themselves up and fasten themselves into coats that neither breathe nor can be easily removed. But for the practicality of a poncho! Easy on, easy off. Tossed back like a scarf for a little fresh air. Nothing on earth could offer so elegant a solution. And yet there are no ponchos in Paris. Not a single one. A peasant garment, they'd probably say. We prefer sickness and suffocation. We *choose* it. And yet, they are not oblivious to the horrors they impose upon themselves. Not for a moment. Every year, at the beginning of June, they run away and leave this place deserted. Every one of them. I watch them pouring by from the window, mesmerised by their sudden coherence, the philosophical upheaval, a culture of dawdlers simultaneously infuriated in flight. If you didn't know the self-loathing of these people, if you didn't realise that their escape is only imagined, an indulgence, the whole thing would look like a mutual epiphany, like all the fish in a single bowl suddenly learning to fly. But some of us cannot leave, because in fact we are not truly here. They say there's never any end to Paris, but I don't know if there's really a beginning to it either. It's a dream you're having. A dream where little makes sense. A dream or a nightmare. I know that it must be one of these because I've never really lived here. I never even learned to speak French. How can you live somewhere for seventy years and not speak the language? No, it's a fantasy, that's all. A fantasy played out just beyond the *arrondissements*, a little off the map, under a bridge, near a park, behind a fence, through a tunnel, underground, behind a tower, after the café-*tabac*, beside a flagpole, just through the alley and two buildings down on the right. You couldn't find it if you wanted to. When I was young I lived on the other side of the world. Whereas now it is the dream that is monstrous, back then I was a monster lost outside a dream. Perhaps that's how everyone remembers their adolescent years. Years of being terrible, lost and unreal. For a long time no-one looked into my eyes, and so, like you Agent Vell, I found nowhere to register my humanity. The stuff of sympathy, the animal world, they had never claimed me as their own. At thirty years old, unevolved by love, I was still in every sense a child. And so, like a child, I ran away from home. I went to every corner of the world and was accepted nowhere. Cultures gathered and discussed in their own language my presence on the frontier. I could always hear their whispers like swelling storms. Now and then, one brave soldier or mercenary or else a diplomat came across my horizon. At the sight of his sharpened stick and the echo of his animal yelling, I drove myself away before I was reached. I soon learned how to find the margins of everywhere. I don't know how much of this is true. Who really knows if the past is real? Perhaps you know, Agent Vell. Perhaps you are hysterical right now, cavorting privately with the truth. I suspect you are. I can hardly stand to look at you anymore. It kills me. There is something in your writing of recent years that is so perfectly captured by your blank expression, the one you're wearing right now. Condescension, absolutely. But that belongs to your eyes, while on the whole your face, like your words, imposes something further. Something more complex or else more simple. Not a mood, but rather a tone. As ominous as a scream on the other side of a door. A rapping and thumping on the wood, a splitting in the grains. For all my efforts to ignore it, I have not been able to

ward off a growing sense of fear for your subjects, those poor souls
you follow and narrate with the coldness of fate itself. The way
their every gesture, as you describe it, whether it is languid or
hurried, performed in lust or habit, is a gesture that is somehow
sick with panic. I have tried to ignore the howling screams, the
gnashing of the door as the wood begins to give, devising this way
of reading in a state of urgency, as if the words were a brittle suspension bridge whose planks will undoubtedly crumble under my
step and which I can cross only by running breathlessly and light-
footed. I don't know why I explain all this in metaphors, which
I can see now have become increasingly elaborate and also confused. Perhaps it's my mind's way of receding from what worries
me most, a satire of my own fear. It's a childish device, I realise.
But childishness is not such a terrible pretence, I don't think. Once
or twice over the years I have peered out of the bathroom during
Sister Luz's gatherings. I have watched three or four of them, aging
women in soiled habits, making themselves as small and inevident
as physically possible, their bodies scrunched up and pressed to
the ground, foetal in fact, utterly silent, as one never remembers
being. This pre-human posture is the one in which they offer themselves to my wife's memory. My wife, who it shames me to say you
really do not remember. She was the one who used to hover around
you like an aura, needle in hand, as though you were some kind
of plaything that had gotten old. The one who used to set before
you soup after soup, only to have it go cold, untouched, under your
chin. The one who, before you arrived and after you departed, and
ultimately while you were still here, knelt constantly on the floor
beneath us, under this very table, flipping possessed through book
after book. The one who hadn't spoken to me in thirty or so years
leading up to her death, except for the one day, many years after
she had given up attending to you, when she crawled out from
under the table only to say that we should not call you Pierre anymore. Alarmed by her emergence from terminal silence, I asked

her then what we should call you instead. As she disappeared back under the table I heard her mutter "Ancient Hell" and my stomach twisted in pain or else fright, so that I scampered at once to the bathroom in bodily confusion. I sat on the toilet thinking about how old you might really be, and beginning to understand what consecutive lifetimes will do to the soul. I'd never heard her say anything so horrible before. It was only a few years later that I realised that I had misheard her, and that the name she'd given you was actually "Agent Vell." And at that moment my stomach twisted even more tightly, sending me once again to the bathroom. I had been thinking at the time that your writing could no longer be described as actions, or literary sketches, or even prose. The last semblance of poetry had long been drained from your notebooks. You had become an author of reports. Reports—the form of condescension. The rhetorical manifestation of your face and its empty tone. The output of a machine. If a poem, Agent Vell, is a dance and a risk, then a report is a march and a certainty. A military march. That is why I was so moved when I understood my wife's final designation for you. A perfect title. It was her recognition of your ignorance to her affection, your inability to register her motherly kindness, to embrace her with your eyes, just once, so that she could see the history of the world, and have some means to forgive you. She was fifteen when I met her, Agent Vell, somewhere on the vague road I followed on my way to here. Somewhere in the netherland between cultures. A tiny, beautiful, Japanese doll who inexplicably fixed herself to me, as a single fly sometimes pesters one for hours at a time. She brought as an offering the thing that no-one before her had thought to bring, the most obvious thing, the perfect thing, which I put on my face at once and have never again removed. I lost my virginity to her and eventually I would ruin her utterly. I know what you're thinking. After fifty years of suffering in this apartment she looked neither particularly beautiful, nor Japanese. Her contempt for me was virtually her only feature by the time of her death.

I have made a point of never trading in philosophies, Agent Vell, especially with someone like you, for whom there can be no wisdom. But let me tell you something I'm sure of, not because it's wise but because it's relevant to understanding my poor wife. There are only two sincere gestures of which humans are capable: a minute of self-immolation, and a lifetime of contempt. Everything else is contrivance. I can assure you that my wife's contempt was as sincere as death. Excuse me, Agent Vell. Please do excuse me if I pass wind like that from time to time. I'm not lacking in manners, as you know. A soul, perhaps. Manners, no. The thing is that I don't feel it coming, don't notice the wind passing. I only hear the sound as it leaves, as though from someone else's person. It usually precedes a change in temperature, the way a cat perceives a storm. And there it is again, sure as death, right on cue, another cold snap. As sudden as a swarm of bees blocking out the sun. Bear with me while I grab the milk. I'll just lean on your shoulder again, if you don't mind. At my age the weather is a mood but it's also a pain. A pain in my joints, to be precise. Do you know that when she died my wife's knees were fused into hunks of unmovable bone and muscle and nerve? Two huge male nurses tried to pry open the impenetrably clenched jaw that each of her legs had become, grunting and sweating, manipulating her from every angle with their giant, bloodless hands. How I blocked my ears at the sound of every joint and bone inside her, everything but her knees, seemingly snapping or else dislocating under duress. I can hardly bare to recall those animals, with shoulders like mountains and heads like boulders, as they wrestled pitifully with her colossal contempt. They seemed not to understand how small this apartment is. There were books falling down all over the place, like the building was rapidly caving in, or else melting. The table was turned over and pressed against the window. All to no avail. They carried her out exactly as they'd found her, on her knees indeed, like a Buddhist statue, the body-bag merely drawn over her head. And it was so that Sister Luz, at that time a young and desperate and frightened nurse in the local morgue, a university student and effectively a child, saw my dear wife for the first and last time, the frightening human image that would become the centre of her tiny faith. I've come to understand, Agent Vell, that our souls do not really wear our bodies, but that rather our bodies wear our souls. My wife's contempt became her and could not be separated from her, not by the strength of a thousand giant men. I, too, am evidence of this. As a child I was unimaginably cruel, and my face was trans-formed, in one perfect instant, into the very image of my terrible soul. At my school there was a little girl, one year younger than myself, who began to grow whiskers under her nose. She started to look like a cat, or else a mouse. She had always had a small, raw, upturned pink nose. I decided to steal a single whisker, for what exact reason I don't know. One day I followed her into a park. In the seclusion of many thick trees, I pinned her down on the grass and tried to pluck a whisker from her upper lip. I had thought it would be simple, a moment of childish curiosity, or else that's how I am tempted to retell it. In my hands the whiskers felt as fat as quills, and I became enraged as my fingers constantly slipped off them, like tweezers that refused to take a splinter. She writhed terribly beneath me, with strength that seemed beyond her, her screams muted in my hand. But I could not have one. Not that day, nor the next. Nor for a whole week after. Every day leading up to the acci-dent I followed her to the park and descended upon her. I silenced her with my hand, plucked and yanked at her whiskers until pink foam formed at the corners of her mouth, or else her freckled belly convulsed enough to scare me away. I should add, Agent Vell, that I use that word, the word *accident*, to describe the event itself and not what happened to me personally, which was something alto-gether perfectly intended and executed. But there were those who really did die that day accidentally, or else collaterally. Others were more complexly implicated, such as my father, whose own death was a horrible mistake and a terrible injustice, but whose subsequent non-existence was precisely contrived as my fair dues. Thereafter I wore my soul and people saw it and ran away at the sight and the thought of me. Then there were the freaks and weirdos who took me in to satisfy a fetish, while others used me as though to challenge their own humanity, which are really the same thing in the end. Only I knew that it was perfect justice, all of it. Every paranoid flinch, every sinister embrace. I had condemned myself to receiving the worst of human interactions, those performed in fear, sickness and pity. My own mother, once a small, athletic and lively woman, grew suddenly bloated and old and hunched, in order that she should not have to look up at my face any more. She came to resemble a giant mole, her gaze affixed to her own feet. When it came to finding ways of evading me, human cunning proved to be a bottomless well. And yet my own shame refuses to remind me of its presence to this day, even for a moment. Though I have worn this mask for so long now that even I recognise it as my own face, still I cannot disguise this ellipse of teeth-marks in my palm. Take a look. Play author to your eyes for just one moment, Agent Vell, I beg you. The impressions have not risen, as though it was only a second ago that I pulled my hand out of that little girl's mouth and ran like a coward through the trees. Look, Agent Vell. Look, if you're in there, Pierre. The skin is not broken, there is no scar tissue, and yet the flesh will not forget. Perhaps one hundred years is just a second in the life of a soul. Perhaps it is only moments ago that she squirmed a flattened shape into the grass beneath me. Sometimes when I am reading I find myself staring into my own palm, and the warmth of panicked breath seems present there still. Since the death of my wife I must have read ten thousand books, perhaps many more than that. Do you know, Agent Vell, that ever since I won the deeds to those apartments in Rome, every single page I have turned has brought my whole being to the point of unimaginable suspense? Every time I feel my finger slide under the upper right-hand corner of the page that follows, my heart levitates toward my throat. And every time so far I have turned the page and the suspense has dispelled into nothing. One day, I infinitely dread, I will find between the pages of one of these books the three slips of paper that are those ill-fated deeds. And then the moment will come where I will turn the book over and look at the cover, and at that time I will know just how cruel I am. Will I be confronted, in a horrible flash, with the recognition of the place where I hid them, from my wife and also from my own consciousness, those many years ago? Will I remember then that this horrible life was really my masterpiece, contrived for reasons of selfishness and cruelty? Or will I in fact turn it over and feel nothing, the negative emotion of a face or a place unrecognised, and know that the author of my wife's contempt, the gnarling of her knees and her existence, was not some buried faction of my terrible self, my teeth-marked soul? Will I know then that this, too, was *your* doing? I look around at these walls and see the millions of books that will remain unread. This apartment, Agent Vell, was once big enough for us to play host. Not only for you and I and my wife kneeling under the table. Not only a handful of old expatriate Mexican pilgrims squeezed knee-to-knee into the clearing on the floor to pray to a strange idol. Did I ever mention that Sister Luz was once known as Martha Marie-Orlando, and that she was working at the mortuary on the day my wife's body was received? Perhaps I have, or perhaps I have not. In any case, this apartment was once big enough for a dozen guests to visit and to sit in comfort. A small party, perhaps. Not that anyone ever came besides you. But as you can see, every wall is now lined with books to the last inch and crevice. And even those alone would be a great many. But I see the layers behind those that are visible. Four, five, even six layers of books in some places. A crust you could sit inside of. A sort of insulation, an insect's winter nest. A fungus that I have cultured over many years. When we first came to Paris I went out in the day looking for work and for money. But I only ever came home with books, books in my native English. Except on the very rare occasion, I never brought more than one or two back at a time. What is the effect of one book on the space of an apartment? It's negligible, really. A handful of sand tossed on the beach. My wife would turn her gaze at me each time I returned, and then she would glance at the one or two books in my hands, and she would say nothing. Even her eyes, which were growing dull, said very little. Her eyes were like the quiet click of a machine that registers infinitesimal things. I never found a real job, of course, because I never spoke French. On Sundays I would clean some windows, or else walk all the way to Rue Mouffetard where a group of English women met for tea. I sat with them and they fed me the scraps from their plates and side-dishes. Sometimes, when they stayed in the café for lunch and champagne, one of them might take me up to her apartment and send me home with a couple of books as well as some money. Though I never said much at all, they had convinced themselves that I was a struggling artist. I was not in a position to rebuke their charity. It seemed to please them to talk about how they'd all determined to protect and nurture me and be the mothers to my creations. Though in fact, when it came down to it, none of them ever gave me more money than was enough to buy a small bottle of milk, or else a tatty old book. There was also a bakery down near the canal whose kneading machines I'd clean for bread. As well, the black hairdressers up near Gare du Nord paid me a little to sweep up and dump the cuttings from the floors of their shops and the sidewalk. But however I made some money or food I rarely came home with anything but books. If I was not gifted one, I would buy it from a second-hand shop or else one of the few market stalls that kept books in English. And at the time I never actually read very much. That's the thing that really lit the fire of contempt in my wife's eyes. I'm sure of it. I was going out in the day with the pretence of earning us money to escape from Paris, but returning instead with books, which were merely bricks. Every afternoon for many decades I'd return to the apartment with one more brick, or else a couple of bricks, to stack against the walls. My wife was so hateful towards Paris that she never went outside. So it was as though I was doing nothing at all with my life but reducing the space she occupied in the world. And still she said nothing to deter me. She spent her time in the clearing on the floor, which had shrunk until there was hardly enough room for her to stand. And then one day I came home and did not see her there. I noticed her foot emerging from under the edge of the table, like the tail of a cornered rat. It frightened me. I turned around at once. I ran back to the café on Rue Mouffetard and sat with the ladies for hours. I sat in silent agitation until they all got up and went their ways. When they dispersed around the various arterial streets that ran off the avenue, I followed one in particular. She always wore colours like blue or green or jasmine, and not the forest but the ocean shades of them. In an alley I called out and ran up to her and said that I needed to escape from Paris. She looked at me as if she knew everything, a look of misplaced reverence and undue respect and also pity. She said there was a way but that it was as terrible as the look of panic in my eyes. She told me to go back to my apartment and wait. She asked if I had a wife and I said yes, I did. She said, make sure your wife is fast asleep. I won't go into everything in detail, Agent Vell. That night was the kind that one locks away. I had thought it would be easy to gamble with my life, since I was not much pleased with it. But I had retained that feeble instinct that trades every vanity for survival, which is perhaps yet another vanity. Would that my wife was not fast asleep under my feet, I'd have cried at impossible volumes. I know well that none of this is news to you, Agent Vell. You have ridden alongside the omen of death in the privileged or else cursed chariot of narration. Or rather, that was how I thought of you until recently, in my naivety. But I know now that you and the omen occupy the same seat, crack the same whip, and brandish the same weapons. Did you ever wonder why it is that I make a fuss of shuttling the milk back and forth whenever you are here? Yes, for one, because temperature fluctuations are to milk's ultimate detriment. That's as true as the sun and moon. But also because I want to make a quick lap of you, a survey, to make an account of what you are carrying. It took me some time to understand why someone like you should need a gun. The day I first noticed it, there on the table, under your giant palm, I was thrown into a state of complete confusion. But I became used to it, in a sense. Everyone is entitled to defend himself. Then a few years ago I saw the second gun, on your ankle, visible because your trousers leg had become caught on its handle. The shaft itself was as thick as a man's arm. There's nothing defensive about a gun like that, Agent Vell. And just two or three months ago I noticed that your belt buckle was not what it had seemed, but instead a huge pair of scissors, gleaming silver, that look as though they could castrate a bull. Look now, there it is again, I have teardrops falling onto my thighs. My eyes must be making them. Well, there's nothing to do but sit it out I suppose. A few minutes at most. I remember waking on that fateful morning, still seated at the table, my wife dozing in ignorance underneath me. The deeds were right there, laid out like a triptych. I woke up my wife by shaking her with my feet. And then I got down onto my knees and tried to lift her up, but she seemed to have grown as heavy as lead. That's when I looked into her weary eyes and told her what had happened, not all the details, but most. Not that I had spent all night seated above her with two old Chinese ladies, rakish as mantises, so similar they must have been twins, the table strewn with fruit and dusty bottles of Bordeaux, and a pistol whose mirrored handle seemed to crunch like shattered glass as they took turns raising it with their spindly wrists. How they kissed and petted each other and fed me broken biscuits and fruit like a parrot. How I turned my back on the wild animal of fate as though it were some docile pet. How I returned every prize to the centre of the table, transforming one coin into

a few bills, two bills into a diamond the size of a knuckle, a diamond into a deed, one into two, two into three. How I would have
gone on forever if not for the fact that those wiry insects began to
whisper amongst themselves that I was some kind of demon, a
bearer of bad luck, that it was best to leave me with those three
deeds and be gone forever. I hardly need to tell you any of this,
though, do I Agent Vell? You can surely recall it as well as I can.
You knew I would have gone on until the inevitable. You knew
that I was ultimately a man of cowardice, looking for a way out.
You gave me a streak that saved my life, the most unmerciful of
things. You sent those insects running in fear of me, happy to
leave behind just a few deeds, a pittance, the price of their souls.
That was the first time I knew for sure that you had stolen something from me. Get up now, I said to my wife. Go into the bathroom
and wash your face. When you return you will see that I have found
a way for us to leave Paris, finally. She didn't move from her lightless hovel, didn't take my hand, didn't blink. I reached up to the
table and gathered the deeds and brought them down to show her.
She stroked them with her fingers, which were getting crooked
already, but were still so pretty to look at, like a child's fingers, fat
and pink at the tips. She crawled slowly out from under the table
like an animal that hears its food falling into a bowl, and went over
to the doorway and put on a hat. Then she walked out of the apartment and I lay my head on the table, which, at that moment, was
like a wafer-thin sheet of ice under which laid the oceanic abyss of
sleep. The exhaustion of the night past sat its million tonnes on my
temple. I already knew that my wife would return with two tickets
to Rome, that upon her return the deeds would be missing, and that
they would remain so forever, that her existence from that moment
on would be spent on her knees, back under this table, turning
over every page of every book in this apartment, searching for those
deeds. All I would ever see of her again was an occasional hand
reaching out to swap one book for another. I would continue

nonetheless to go out into Paris and return with books that I would not read until after her death, as though I were preparing for a kind of hibernation. Sometimes it was the second, third, or fourth copy of the same unread book. Handfuls of hay to add to her mountainous stacks, so to speak. And no horse in sight. Nonetheless I dared to think fleetingly about Paris, the dream that was almost over, a thought that I knew was dangerous at that moment. And it was then that the ice broke under the weight of my head and everything in it and the water rose up and swallowed me. I fell at once into this complex dream, or else many dreams, the consequence of which is really a kind of exponential dream: I see you at the table. I'm returning from the bathroom. I am wet. I pretend that I was not expecting you, but I was. I am. I am always expecting you. I am only surprised when I emerge from the toilet and you are not there. I'm emerging and you're there, that's how I know it goes. But I am condemned ever to recognise you as merely an omen, as a sign of something for which you are only a warning, a state of naivety to which I am eternally returned. Over and over again, until the end of time, I must learn that this is not really the case, or else it is no longer the case. That lesson is my lot. I walk to my chair beside you at the table. But then I wake behind the door again, seated on the toilet, and I haven't emerged, not really. I'm ten or twenty seconds behind myself, which prepares me but does not make me less frightened or morbidly sad that I know exactly what's coming. It is this sadness and fatefulness that brings me to tears, tears which gush as only a dream will allow, and seeing them, soaked by them, I realise that I am still there, inside the dream, or perhaps assumed by more than one dream, some of which are not my own, caught in a sort of Venn diagram in which the overlapping territory of many dreams forms a small, complex shape. There is a moment in which I must leave and also must not leave the bathroom, a paradox of certainties that threatens everything, until suddenly something unnameable, some pulse of impatience or else intelligence that is too potent or else momentarily too stubborn or excited to be satiated from within the peaceful torment of that oddly-shaped moment, like some living act that lunges out of a dream, a half-phrase shouted at a moment of waking, a fist thrown at a phantom but received by a pillow, something of this very nature urges me up from the toilet and out of the door, soaking wet or otherwise, and I begin my worn excuses, apologies, claims of surprise, greetings. Good morning. Or is it afternoon?

7

ARTHUR WAYNE BOYD walked down to the staff carpark at five o'clock the next morning. He drove to his apartment in Elizabeth North and showered and went to bed. When he woke in the afternoon, he went to his desk and opened a notepad and wrote, virtually without pause, for eight hours. At five o'clock that afternoon he stood and circled his bedroom. He looked down at the two filled booklets. They were closed and stacked and topped with a pen. The pen's hexagonal shaft was impressed upon his finger, which he rubbed with the tip of his thumb.

For the next two-and-a-half years he was busy, unflinchingly, at his doctorate.

Art continued to work four graveyard shifts per week at Lady Flinders Home for the Elderly, Elizabeth East. It was during those two-and-a-half years that he stopped wearing exclusively dark clothes. He also stopped gelling his hair into a Mohawk and powdering his face and wearing eyeliner. He threw away the tiny rag-like black shirts that he used to fasten around himself with safety pins and through which you could usually see a nipple. His studded belts went to the Salvation Army. He put the black boots that laced high and had massive soles away in a box that he never looked in again. He took out his piercings and the holes in his ears, nose, stomach, and nape started to fill in. For a while he maintained a little hair on his chin and a moustache but otherwise he shaved every morning. He cut his hair off and then grew it long enough to tie it up at the back in a neat ponytail. These changes did not feel like an expression of anything in particular, not to him. The only society he kept was with the mostly older lady nurses at the home. They hardly noticed this radical change in Art. He'd always obeyed the codes of dress at work, wearing the uniform and taking out his piercings and combing his hair aside neatly. The only thing to change in the minds of the nurses was that he'd filled out a bit. He'd become more talkative, too. Some of them said that he looked happier. For a while he'd been sleeping with an undergraduate who worked in the coffee shop on campus. But they decided they didn't have the time for each other.

Art presented his research to a full theatre at the University of Queensland, Brisbane, in August, 1993. He was asked then to re-present his work, which had since been critically amended, at a conference on major post-WWII writers held in Christchurch, New Zealand, in November of the same year. The reception he received on these two occasions affected Art acutely. In Brisbane, the applause overwhelmed him. He feigned sickness to avoid the dinner function which some colleagues that he didn't really know had organised for him. Instead he took a taxi to the serviced apartment where he was staying in Auchenflower. He sat in the shower for hours, crying. In Christchurch, Art had arranged to meet a man he had been calling on the phone during an intense period of editing. The man was a winemaker. He came to the presentation to see Art. After-wards, he and Art went out for coffee and then to Art's hotel, where they shared a bottle of wine and had intercourse. After the wine-maker had gone home, Art cried again. The applause that he had received at the presentation two days earlier was still ringing in his ears.

ART DID NOT ENJOY the communal aspect of academic life. He felt unsuited to it. He had made no real friends during his undergrad-uate degree and treated his PhD mentor with strict formality. He enamoured himself to no-one with whom he shared research. After his fellow academics stopped applauding his work, they also stopped contacting him. He was offered no chairs or posts of any kind. When it occurred to Art that he would have to work to continue his academic career as hard as he had worked to launch it, he at once decided to abandon it altogether. He accepted a management position at Lady Flinders, which occupied him almost completely.

The next year, for a week following his thirty-second birthday, Art took annual leave and went to see Uluru. There he experienced the first apparent spiritual change in his life. At the time he was sleeping with three different men on a monthly basis, two of whom he slept with as a couple (which is to say that Art was one part of a threesome). He also was sleeping with a woman from Mount Barker who he'd met through a phone service, and who came down to visit him most weekends. She was a dominatrix and she arrived in a rusty yellow Volkswagen with a suitcase of things with which she would brutalise Art. Everyone Art slept with was intelligent with respect to Art's definition of it (i.e. intelligence). For Art there really could be no attraction without some intellectual chemistry. Creativity was a kind of intelligence that Art could respect, as was wit. But they had to be of the *right* kind. In which sense he thought of all expressions of intelligence as having their own peculiar character, like a face. Intelligence could be pretty, comforting, repulsive, and a great many other things. It could be almost anything except truer or else more definitive than another, just as a face could not be such things. Two of the men he slept with were store owners, another was a gardener, and the dominatrix was an English as a Second Language teacher.

The morning on which Art was supposed to climb Ayers Rock, before the sun had entirely risen, he was bitten by a black snake and flown to a hospital in Darwin. He experienced two hallucinations while flying over the desert in the emergency helicopter. In one of these hallucinations, the snake that had bitten Art was still attached to his leg, and no-one was helping him to remove it (the latter part of which statement is obviously true both inside and outside of the hallucination). Art looked into the snake's eyes and screamed. The snake appeared to look back at him and firm its bite, as though with malice. Without Art being able to describe how it was so in retrospect, the snake's eyes had betrayed to him a sinister nature and intention. Sinister, but also personal. They were like the eyes of a great, disturbing portrait, pursuing the reticence of its viewer. When Art left the hospital, though he had accepted the medical conclusion that everything regarding the snake had been a fantasy, he still believed that, for all intents and purposes, he had seen the face of evil.

The other hallucination was of a small Aboriginal boy, dressed in a pair of torn jeans, without a shirt or shoes. The Aboriginal boy was next to the medic in the helicopter, squatting at the foot of Art's stretcher, looking fixedly down at Art. He never moved. But Art knew by looking at his eyes that the boy was trying to escape, desperately, fearfully wishing not to be there with Art, and really considering the idea of jumping out of the large opening on the helicopter's flank. Art had wanted to reach up and grab the boy to stop him from hurting himself. But at the same time he realised that *he* was what the boy was afraid of. The boy stared at him as though nothing in the world were so terrible. To Art's mind, the eyes of both the snake and the boy were like hallucinations within the hallucinations.

The other peculiarity, perhaps the most difficult for Art to later reconcile, was that the two hallucinations had never overlapped; the snake and the boy did not in any way interact. Each had been in the helicopter from take-off to landing. Each set of eyes had seen him enter and depart the cabin. It was as if Art had experienced them in parallel, as if there had been two bitten Art's flying over the desert at the one time. For the rest of his life he could recall them both with incredible clarity.

He never again pretended to use intelligence as a judgment of character.

Art went back to work at Lady Flinders after two months. He had become thinner and had developed grey streaks in his sideburns. A temporary facial tic made him look pensive. During his time away, many of the older nurses and some managers had moved to another Lady Flinders home that had been built in the nearby suburb of Burnside. He was now second-in-charge and there were seven new nurses. Only one staff member had been there longer than Art. Her name was Jennifer, and in fact it was she who had got him the job at Lady Flinders some years ago now. She had been doing a Masters in European Literature at the time and Art had met her in one of the second-hand bookstores on Hindley Street. Both were looking for Günter Grass books. Art was searching for *Local Anaesthetic* and Jennifer for *Cat and Mouse* (indeed, they were not only both looking for Günter Grass books, but looking for books from the same era, and specifically for the dusted gold/bronze Penguin editions that had been issued in the seventies). Having majored in psychology during her undergraduate degree, Jennifer was occasionally asked to examine guests at Lady Flinders, and to provide reports in secret to the director. This strictly unofficial role was not known to Art until many years later. Jennifer was four years younger than Art and on that day, which he remembered well, she wore jeans and a baby-blue Polo shirt, and as such he thought she'd been to a private school, probably Wilderness or Loreto. But though they looked deeply mismatched, she was not obviously put out by the way Art used to dress at the time. They went for coffee but there was nothing romantic in it. After Jennifer's reference had got him the job, Art bought her a bottle of whiskey and gave her a second edition of Camus' *The Fall*. This gesture had neatly rounded off any upward trajectory in their relationship. At the time she was seeing a boy who was a medical intern.

Back then Art used to read all through the nightshift, between his half-hourly rounds. On a good night he could get through three hundred or so pages without distraction. It was really the heartbeat of his academic life. After the security guard waved to him through the glass windows to say he was headed home, at around eleven, Art would masturbate in the staff toilet. Most often he masturbated while thinking of the other nurses who worked at Lady Flinders. The relative age of the majority of them didn't bother Art. His appetite for imagining new nooks and crannies of the building where he would unburden himself in the mouth or on the chest or back of one of those older women was insatiable. Different parts of the home seemed to suit different nurses. Inevitably the role of all of them in his fantasies was one of suffering under an inexhaustible desire for Art and his potent sexuality. He liked the idea of being passionately resisted by someone who ultimately needed and indeed actively wanted him to the extent of cruelty. His violence was assumed by them and reflected in their own masochism. The brutality of these fantasies was, to Art's mind, a normal aspect of their being fantastical, the way size is categorical in dreams. He expected that all honest sexual fantasies would sound ridiculous and possibly psychotic out loud. Otherwise, what was fantastic about them?

Art began to feel attracted to Jennifer after returning from the hospital in Darwin. She had never come into his fantasies before. She was now in her late twenties. He felt nervous and shy when she came to his office, which was at the back of the east wing, looking over a park that the rubbish truck backed up to in the morning. One evening he told her how he felt about her. Her response was collected and seemingly prepared, as though he'd asked her a few times already. She said that they could date, that she had been hoping they would someday, but she had rules. Then she began to list her rules, which included the minimum time before they would be able to sleep together (six days) and the maximum time he would be allowed to date her without proposing (ten months) after which she declared that she would be actively and guiltlessly seeking other partners. That evening she went home and slept with Art. They never even ironically mentioned the rules again.

Art and Jennifer didn't become a couple. But they became very close. Thereafter, Art actually looked forward to coming to work. Ostensibly, so did Jennifer. Jennifer was still studying a Masters, only she had changed her course to Philosophy and was taking the lightest possible workload. She never talked about it and seemed to Art to be doing it out of a waning desire for something that probably escaped her even now. She talked a lot about her family, who were not wealthy in the way Art had imagined. Her father was a truck driver and her mother worked in a chemist. Jennifer lived with a young female student in the centre of the city, down an alley that ran off Rundle Mall. She was very sure that this would be her last year at university. She and Art talked a lot about the possibility of his finding for her a full-time position at Lady Flinders. That September, Art's father died. The service reminded Art of his grandfather's funeral, at which Art had seen his own father cry for the first time. It was there as a thirteen-year-old boy that Art had realised he could, with a little concerted effort, stop himself from crying, even when the Last Post played over the silent field, each change of note seeming to test him, pulling physically at his gut. But it could be resisted. And from this realisation he had understood that if it was possible not to cry then it was not necessary to cry. Art's father had left his mother in 1983 and moved to Port Pirie. As well as buying car wrecks for a yard, he had helped his new partner's father grow contract grapes. Art had only seen him a few times since then and each time they had gone to a restaurant in the city where Art ate cheese doorstops and toast with pâté. Once they saw *The Hunt for Red October*. Art's father would always pay.

Jennifer attended the funeral with Art. It was a windy day. There were very few headstones in the part of the cemetery where Art's father was buried, and the bright lawn rolled like a field and felt to them both like a golf course. It was a Saturday and they could feel the rumbling in the ground from a racing track whose tower they could see in the distance. After the funeral, Art played Bocce with some men who had known his father as well as the children of his father's partner. The men did not recognise Art, who they had known as a black-eyed, pierced and studded youth. Jennifer asked Art a few days after the funeral if she could write a story about it. She'd already given up on study and he could tell she was anxious about her free time.

Art visited his mother a few times after his father's death. She had amassed a large family from her second marriage. She lived in West Torrens, in the house where Art had grown up. Art showed Jennifer the hole in the front yard where the water meter was. As a child he and his friends used to cover the hole with leaves and try to trick each other into falling in. He lifted the loose red bricks in the fence and found the stuffing of lolly wrappers and paddle-pop sticks; he used to think the redback spiders could be trapped that way. Art's mother was the absolute matriarch of the other family, which was fanatical about football. One of them was a professional, training with a Melbourne team. Art's mother was always wearing the yellow and blue scarf or vest of the local club, whose games she was taken out to watch every week. She used a wheel-chair, though Art did not know what was actually wrong with her. If she had to use her hands they came slowly out from a little knitted rug on her lap, and shook. She was much older than his father. But for her age she was pretty, and in a way she was youthful. Her skin was pinkish and she had tiny wrinkles around her eyes that made her look happy. She had long grey hair that she wore pinned up or else bundled into a loose beanie in her club's colours.

Jennifer would go along with Art to see her. Art's mother had them walk her along the Torrens River, which was right across her street. There was a two-rowed wall of tall pines along the water's edge which they weaved through on a foot-pestled track in the grass. The dry pinecones cracked or were crushed under the wheelchair's wheels. Jennifer would push Art's mother and Art would hold his mother's hand. She talked a lot about her other family and especially the boy who was playing football in Melbourne. Art sometimes watched the football, but not much. Jennifer's father had apparently been into it, but Jennifer didn't understand it either.

ART PICKED UP JENNIFER one day that December and they decided spontaneously to go to the horse races. They called Art's mother to cancel a visit that they had planned for that afternoon. They sat alone in the top corner of the stands for hours sharing bottles of cheap sparkling wine. The wind and the sun's reflection of the empty steel seats in front of them slowly burned their faces. That night they went back to Art's place and slept together. The next day was overcast and they stayed in and read the newspapers and watched television. In the afternoon they had a bath. After that they planned no more trips to see Art's mother. They called her on Christmas.

In the first week of January, Art flew to Christchurch and met up with the winemaker. Art had been calling him a couple of times a year, usually on weekends, when he felt his loneliness. At the airport, as they shook hands, the man admitted to Art that he wasn't really a winemaker; he always told lies when he could, though he didn't really know why. He was really a sales representative for a wine wholesaler. It was a small lie, really, but he always had to say something untrue. It was a part of who he was. His name was Thomas Cullen, and he was now sixty-five years old. He was thickly set, with a barrel chest and a white beard like an older Hemingway. Thomas had contracted AIDS sometime after last seeing Art. He was pretty sure he knew who had given it to him but he was even more sure that the person would be impossible to find. He and Art decided to drive up the east coast toward the top of the South Island. Art had rented a Mercedes.

They stopped for a few days in Marlborough, where they ate a lot of seafood and tasted wines. They slept in a small, spare room

in the house of Thomas' brother. Thomas' brother was younger
than Thomas but still significantly older than Art. He had a young
wife and a daughter. The wife was part Maori and had a tattoo on
one side of her neck, and the daughter, who was three years old,
looked Chinese. Together the four of them ate lunches that became
dinners. Everything Thomas and his brother said to each other was
underlined by a complex and sometimes poetic discourse of taste
in which Art managed to find enjoyment and even to participate
without ever really knowing what they were talking about. Thomas
would get up from time to time and circle the table, kissing every-
body. They let him hold the baby if she was still awake. At night,
while Thomas slept in the other of two single beds, Art could hear
the couple making love upstairs. The part Maori woman was incredibly beautiful. He saw her tattoo in a dream, crawling.

One night Art woke up and Thomas was kneeling at the side
of his bed, his forehead suppliantly knocking against Art's hip. A
ribbed, white singlet stretched across his thick, silver-haired back
like some sort of harness. He was crying profusely but soundlessly.
Art thought long and hard about patting Thomas' bald head but
in the end he remained frozen, pretending to be asleep.

They arrived in Nelson on the second-last day of Art's trip. They
spent the afternoon touring the vineyards. Thomas spoke constantly
of another region, where he said the best wines were made. It was
at the southern end of the island and there was no way they could
get there if Art was going home the next day. Thomas seemed to be
building some kind of wall between them, setting it up and giving
Art a sledgehammer and making him stare at it. He wanted Art to
acknowledge that he didn't need to go home. Art asked what the
place looked like. With a wry grin, staring not back at Art but
straight through the windscreen, Thomas said it was nothing like
where they'd been. It was flat and barren, dry and hopeless. Art
thought long and hard about offering to sleep with Thomas, but
something other than the fear of infection stopped him from doing

so. It was nonetheless a decision of self-preservation. There was a lot of silence on the last day. Thomas asked if they could masturbate together, just looking at each other. Art, who had never felt so acutely sad in all his life, shook his head. On the drive back to Christchurch, Art told Thomas about the experience he had had at Uluru. He tried to impart some of the spiritual effect that the hallucinations had had on him. Thomas seemed like the right person to tell, the only person. Thomas listened seriously, and in the end he asked how Art's life had changed since the experience. Art asked what he meant. Was Thomas asking if he felt different? Thomas said there was no point, obviously, in trying to explain how it feels to live or, therefore, how it might feel different to live differently. He meant, how Art's life had changed, his actual, day-to-day life, or else his spiritual life, since the experience. Art thought about it and said that it hadn't, really, except that he had been promoted in his job. Thomas asked Art what he meant then when he had said it had been a spiritual experience. The question was rhetorical, thought Art.

JENNIFER HAD WON A COMPETITION in the *Advertiser* for the story that she had written about Art's father's funeral. Another two of her stories were being published in student journals in England. She moved in with Art but set herself up in the spare room. Some days they were lazily romantic, like an old couple. Some days they acted like roommates. She slept in his room once every couple of weeks and they didn't necessarily sleep together on those nights. She bought him a very expensive perfume for his birthday. One weekend he drove up to Mount Barker to see the dominatrix. When he came home he went into Jennifer's room and found her writing at her desk. The room seemed to gasp when he opened the door, as though the atmosphere in there had diverged from the rest of the house, like a humid underground chamber.

They lived so for two years. Art was promoted to director of Lady Flinders. Jennifer had scaled back her hours and finally stopped working there altogether. When she told him one day about the psychological reports she used to write occasionally for the director, Art searched among the guests' files. He never found one, though of course he realised they wouldn't have been signed anyway, since they were secret. Art paid all their bills and never once had an idea to challenge the way it was. Jennifer still lived in the second bedroom. She developed a kind of palsy in her right hand and learned to write with her left. He knew nothing about it until one Saturday he realised she brought their coffee cups to the table in two trips. During racing season they went sometimes to Morphettville and sat in the stands. Jennifer drank wildly, with a certain determination, and they would come home in the afternoon and sleep together. It had become a tradition of theirs to go out for lunch on Sunday to a bakery in North Adelaide and then walk to the park at the end of the street and watch the children play on the swings and slides.

One Friday night Art went out to Hindley Street and drank at a bar full of students. He was bald across the top now and wore a moustache, which had a red tinge. There had been a cricket game at the Oval and everyone else on the sidewalks seemed to be dressed in green and gold. The many painted faces yelled and waved streamers taped to toilet rolls in Art's face. At eleven he went into a strip club and sat at the bar. A girl came and sat on his lap. She was tall and young and had a pretty face. He could smell the metal of her large hoop earrings. She took him to a room behind the stage and he gave her some money. Her nipples were small and very red and looked bitten. Her pelvis was bony and her vagina was completely hairless. He'd never seen that before. It had a taut and delicate quality, like an empty balloon stretched and tightly wrapped around a fist. She put her knees on either side of him on a little couch and began to sway and then to bounce up and down. Art held his hands behind his back. He wrung them together, preparing a culture of

warm sweat in his palms. The little room had that imposed darkness about it, the wooden walls painted black, like those inside the
Ghost Train at the Royal Show that are dressed with stretched-
out cotton wool that looks like spider webs. Her soft, little breasts
swept across his open mouth and his jaw seemed to lock anxiously.
When she turned her face away and arched her back, so that he
could see the corrugations of her ribs stretching and the knotted
tendons stressing in her thighs, he hit her. His nervous strike got
part of her jaw and her throat. Instead of a slap there was a hollow
sound and a distant, dull crack. She looked at him silently. He grabbed her hair and pulled her head to one side. The second time he
struck her cleanly across the temple, and he felt the wet of her eye
on the tip of his finger. She fell to the ground and then tried to lift
herself against one of the walls, which collapsed at once. He jumped
over her and ran toward a lit hallway and took a corner. He heard
the girl yelling. There was a stairwell and then a door to an alley.
He ran up the alley and around a corner and then got into a cab and
went home.

On another occasion he went with a prostitute to a room above
Rundle Mall. He wondered how far it was from the room that Jennifer had used to live in, which room he'd never seen. The prostitute was ten or twenty years older than him. She said she had no
pimp, that this was her own apartment where she lived as a single
woman. Without having to ask him anything she said she would
let him violate her to an extent, and for a price, though she asked
him not to touch her face or her right shoulder or shoulder-blade,
which he could see were wasted of muscle. She went over to a
cupboard and began to undress herself in the mirror; skirt and
top, slip and then bra. She smoked fat-looking cigarettes and had
an awkward body that moved unevenly. Her skin seemed to be
someone else's, someone bigger. The horizontal seams across her
belly and thighs looked like fine stitching or invisible bands. Art undressed, sat for a while looking down at himself, and then dressed

again. He left without explanation. That night he walked to Rymill Park and slept under a tree.

Jennifer published her first novel. It was only ninety-four pages long and the type was large. Art found favourable reviews in a couple of the national newspapers. She had used an androgynous pseudonym that was phonetically very similar to Art's own father's name, and by the use of which Art felt inexplicably mocked and somewhat offended, though he never said anything. By now he was able to admit to himself that he was afraid of her.

In May of 2001, Jennifer told him she was pregnant. The baby was born in December. It was a boy. During the pregnancy, Jennifer's family came to the apartment. Art met her mother and her younger sister. Her sister was only a year younger than Jennifer but she really looked like a child. It was then that Art realised how old Jennifer now looked. At thirty-three she had bristly grey hair and sallow lips and eyes that sat half-open. Jennifer and her mother seemed to get on well. He'd never known them to speak, and he had expected something vast and complicated to have come between them. Jennifer completely resigned to incapacitation. She lay on the couch, growing visibly by the day. For some reason Art knew that it was not the pregnancy that exhausted her—she seemed almost relieved by the distraction of the sickness, moods, and discomfort. Sometimes she would ask him to take her to the horse races. Now they sat on the grass and she drank slowly. She ate a lot of fried foods. Her mother would bring store-bought cakes and pastries to the apartment and it was clear that she didn't cook.

When the baby was born, Jennifer named it after her published novel. Her family thought she was crazy, even sick, and supposed the cause was post-natal depression. After two very heated exchanges in the month following the birth, Jennifer's mother stopped coming to the apartment. A few weeks later her sister said something that Jennifer didn't like and Jennifer berated her viciously in front of Art. The sister never returned either. Six months later, Jennifer's publisher called to tell her that sales of her novel had gone up three-fold upon the translation into French. Jennifer asked Art to marry her and he consented.

The next year Jennifer published another novel and fell pregnant again. She and Art had twin girls. The new novel was published simultaneously in French and English. The reviews were more pro-lific but seemed much less favourable. As far as Art could under-stand from reading the reviews, the subtlety of the first novel had descended into vagary in the second. The latter of these was deem-ed offensive to the readers who had been enamoured with the former. The general tone of the critics seemed to be a kind of impatience, if not sheer disappointment. Despite his education, Art had long ago become entirely detached from literature of any kind. He hadn't read a book in years. He actually felt as though he had read enough for a lifetime, or at least he had prepared such an explanation in case someone ever asked. He half-heartedly read a couple of pages of Jennifer's books on the toilet, but he didn't understand them, or else their meaning did not reveal itself quickly enough. The re-views (which he did read closely) described a sort of matrix that he could not decode, and sales were apparently poor. Art never noticed that this had any effect on Jennifer. The twins were named after the second novel, which was titled differently in French and Eng-lish. The firstborn was given the French name (translated back into English). The names of Art's children were all nouns, and after a while Art realised that they did have a certain tacit connection and were quite plausible as names, when you got used to them.

IN 2003 THERE WAS NO NOVEL, nor a pregnancy. One night after work at Lady Flinders, Art had a car accident and was hospitalised for a month. It was the clear fault of the woman he'd hit. The woman came to visit him a week after the accident and they talked about their lives. Art was forty-one and he had never talked about himself abstractly or even thought about himself as something he could step outside of. At least not for a very long time. The woman was Christian and full of spiritual ideals which she expressed sincerely. She was about the same age as Art and had a very calming effect on him. She saw his ring and asked where his wife was. Art said she was a writer, and a very busy one. He didn't know who was looking after the children. The woman asked Art the names of his children and Art made some up.

Art resigned from Lady Flinders from his hospital bed. He never went back to the office for the few things he'd left behind, including a picture of Jennifer naked, which was laminated and stuck on the underside of some floorboards. Nor did he ever think about the many books he'd left all over the place from his first years there. He couldn't even conceptualise himself as someone with a serious interest in German literature anymore. After resigning, he lay in bed and reconstructed a picture of himself reading and note-taking all night in one of the home's wings. Every time he tried to recall this image it seemed to fade. Eventually, he couldn't recall it at all.

The woman from the crash encouraged Art to make peace with whoever he had been. She knew there was something about his past that he despised or was embarrassed about. She said if there was one thing she could do to make it up to him for almost killing him it was to give him a reason to really live. He'd never thought about the fact that he didn't have a reason to live until then.

On the day he was released Art went home with the woman from the crash. She lived in a cottage in Rose Park and was obviously wealthy. She had a twenty-eight-year-old son who built luxury boats. Art had met him a couple of times in the hospital. There were a number of crosses about the house but not so many as to be imposing. The house had a darkroom where some photos were pegged to a string. The photos were so dry that they were curled up like scrolls. Art was tempted to unroll one but he was worried it would crack like dry bark. The smell of suspended chemicals was subtle but sure.

The son came to see them a few times in the weeks after Art had arrived. He seemed entirely welcoming of his mother's new partner. He and Art stayed up late drinking beer and talking. The son was artificially massive, rippled with muscles that made his arms sit wide from his body and his feet splay as he walked. His hair was shaven on the back and sides and neatly swept across the top. There were constellations of moles across his stubbled temples. He smelled of very spicy cologne and was perpetually moist-looking, always appearing to have just showered. Each time Art saw him, he wore a large, blue, ribbed-cotton jumper with a wide neck-hole that made him look like a sailor. Art quickly forgot the woman's warning not to let her son's drinking get out of hand.

One night Art and the son sat out in the living room on big brown recliners with worn fabric levers, drinking beer and then a bottle of port whose rotted cork had broken off and fallen back inside. There were large, square-panelled windows beside Art that overlooked the little garden and the redbrick path that curved through it toward a tin shed. There was a net of fairylights in a low tree and a mossy, fake pond at its foot. The son began to talk about girls and women he'd slept with, many of them during high school. Art asked him whose darkroom it was and the son said he didn't understand the question; it was a part of the house. The son said that for his eighteenth birthday he and four friends had got a prostitute to do them all together. She laid back and let them take turns for a couple of hours and they all got off a couple of times. He had got her to pretend she was being raped and to struggle while he wrapped his arms around her. The son smelled of resin. That was the smell that Art had been trying to think of since he'd first met him, the smell in behind the cologne. Art asked the son if he'd ever used the darkroom, if he took photos. The son smiled distantly, either to answer in the affirmative without saying yes, or to show his impatience. Another time, recently, he'd done the wife of someone he was building a yacht for. She was his age but the buyer was much older. The son had tied her to a bench and put her down on her knees on a sheet of sandpaper. She couldn't even wriggle that way. After most of the port was gone, Art went to the bathroom. When he returned the son rushed up to him and threw him on the ground. Art had no chance to defend himself. He was knocked out with a few unguarded blows to the head. When he came to moments later, the son told him never to come anywhere near his mother again or he'd be raped and killed. He yelled repeatedly: "Get out of here you ugly little man. Get out of here you ugly little man." As Art stumbled through the streets that night he thought of himself as a kind of caricature, ugly and small and bald, a wretched gnome of almost symbolic pettiness. He walked all night and arrived at home the next morning. As he walked past Jennifer's room he could hear the dull clicking of her keyboard. The next day, a Sunday, he took his three small children and Jennifer to the park in North Adelaide where they ate pasties.

A very strange thing happened to Art when he recovered from the accident and the beating. He began to smell pastry all the time. It was a very strong, freshly-baked odour that left him only when he was asleep and sometimes even permeated his dreams. It was so strong at times that, perhaps by association, he felt hot and claustrophobic, his mouth dry and yeasty, as if he was stuck inside a bakery or a giant oven. Sometimes he woke up soaking wet. The taste and smell of all other foods was drowned out. He never mentioned this to Jennifer. Not that she was likely to pay much attention. But really he kept it to himself because he didn't want her to write anything about it. He'd begun to notice, after continued, sporadic scanning on the toilet or in bed, that her books seemed at times to include him in ways that went beyond even the obvious reference of her pseudonym. Sometimes he had the sense that they had been written from his perspective. For example, the narrator in her second book had called himself "lonely like a cow in a windstorm," which was something Art's grandmother used to say, and which Art had himself said a very long time ago, though he couldn't remember the context. At another time the narrator had thrown a coffee cup at his wife, smashing it on the side of her head, which Art had also done, though it was a long time ago now.

One day while reading the newspaper, Art saw an article about one of Jennifer's books. The article said that her first book had been a prime candidate for the Miles Franklin Award, and her second (whose critical reception had radically changed over just a short while, and was now universally considered by critics to be a superior work) for the Man Booker Prize, as well as some other awards that he'd not heard of. The books were not eligible for these awards, however, because the author's identity had not been revealed. Two days later Art received a phone call from a lawyer who was attempting to settle his father's estate. It seemed absurd to Art to imagine that his father had any kind of estate to speak of, though he had been told already that he was the sole beneficiary of his father's will. Apparently, Art's father had been working at his partner's family's vineyard on a kind of perpetual acquisition agreement. Since his death, his partner's family had been involved in a long legal battle over the portioning of the vineyard. Essentially, they had been trying to decide how much of a share of the vineyard Art's father's eight years of manual labour equated to. Art's father's partner had since passed away, and no-one among the shareholders wished to continue with the vineyard. Ultimately, Art's share was determined to be one-fifth of the property. But if he wished to buy the rest of the family out, they would effectively increase his share to a half.

In March of 2005, Art's wife fell pregnant again. Art told her that they were moving to McLaren Vale, a small town just outside Adelaide that sat on Gulf St. Vincent. He had spent all the money from her book sales and the last of his savings from Lady Flinders on the outright purchase of the vineyard. She made no opposition. The property had a medium-sized, raised house on it that was

suitable for them. The vines were tired and had not been harves-
ted in the vintage just passed. The grapes hung sparingly among
among the overgrown, oft-rotten leaves. The ground was full of
snakes and rats revelling in the fallen, dried-out bunches. Art made
friends with a grower at a pub in the town and asked for his help.
The baby was born in December. The vines were badly damaged
and not suitable for the following vintage either. Then the next year
the vines were attacked by disease and rotted out before harvest
arrived. Art was still overwhelmed by the smell of pastry. He never
told anyone that he could barely smell the wines that other grow-
ers often brought to him as a show of solidarity. Nor could he taste
the ripeness of his own grapes. Instead he tried to make decisions
based on the texture of the seeds as he bit them, which was another trick he'd learned.

Jennifer published a new book in early 2007. Art had no idea
if his wife's career was well-managed. One day that summer he
happened to be in the kitchen when her agent came to the property
and begged her to reveal her identity to the public. The agent said
that Jennifer was just about the most exciting and, some people
believed, the best living Australian writer, and that her anonymity
to this point had created enormous interest. Though ultimately, the
agent explained, anonymity had to be broken. "We could talk about
legacy and trust all day but I'd be talking to a brick wall," she said.
"The point is that there are dollars on the table and we're not pick-
ing them up." That night Art told Jennifer that they'd lost everything on the vineyard and might have to sell it. They had no money.
He asked her if maybe she would give her name to the publisher
of her books, and maybe do a paid interview, if only to collect on
the awards that he knew she'd been considered for, whose prizes
were substantial. She looked at him for not very long and then got
up from the table and said she really didn't give a shit either way.
They had to eat.

ART MORE OR LESS did nothing else of any note ever again, other than to raise his children and look after the vineyard. The grapes were eventually good enough to be sold on, though never for a price much above a base rate. Once, after hurting his back in the vineyard, Art lay in bed and read Jennifer's first trilogy in its entirety over four days. The first two books he read twice each. The third did not demand him to do the same. After he'd finished he walked out of his room and went to the spare room, where Jennifer still slept. He could hear the familiar clicking of her keyboard through the door. He'd finally decided to have his say, though the analytical language of his university days had all but left him. He wanted to tell her how reading her three books was like having something very subtly tied to you and then suddenly realising that the thing attached to you is an explosive, and then not being sure if the explosive has gone off already, if you'd already suffered. If that made sense. Or maybe it was like thinking you are alone in a room, and then realising that you *are* the room, and that the lonely thing in the middle is something else, or some essential part of you that you have, perhaps wrongly, been treating as merely discrete. He really didn't want to end up just saying that she was clever, or that he loved the "twist" in her trilogy. He knew, by something like instinct, that she didn't want to hear that.

8

BRIEFLY THERE IS A SORT OF grille of light coming from the right of screen, a few distended glowing bars folding over the side of what looks to be a bed, which hints at the space being a kind of jail or else a cage. (Although, these lights could well be the afternoon sun passing through a series of louvres, though the louvres would have to be vertical, mind you.) The focus is not quite sharp. Suddenly the camera whips to the left, as though accidentally bumped, passing over what looks to be a reclined form on the bed. Briefly you can see a dark bookcase, now well out of focus. Then there's a strange moment where the perspective leers back before dropping hurriedly, a sort of *human* gesture, like, imagine a first-person account of someone drunkenly falling, or maybe of someone being shot in the back. Or—*no*, you know what it looks like?—it looks like the perspective of someone being whipped while fastened to the stocks, the wooden restraints like you see in Westerns or Roman epics or period films set in the Middle Ages, the restrained head rising in shock and pain before sagging again, hopelessly. Maybe the guy's been whipped a hundred times already and he's not really alive anymore. I'm not sure if that's illustrative or helpful to you, when I say that. Anyway, in my professional opinion, I guess the screw which keeps the camera head upright has come loose, or else whoever's shooting has tripped over awkwardly and tried to grab the camera on the way down. That would explain the last dip. But it's a bit more difficult to understand exactly how the whole series of manoeuvres, beginning with the sudden pan to the left, could have happened. Or *why* it happened. In any case, there's now an almost entirely dark, softly textured image, which has to be an unfocussed picture of carpet. The camera's obviously on the ground now. There are some low murmurings going on but generally the sound has that sort of internal quality, like someone underwater, or like when you stop your ears and can hear things inside yourself. Then the sound (of the film) cuts out completely, and soon after the image follows.

That's it for a while.

My guess is that it's just one of those things where the cameraman has forgotten to turn off the camera, and maybe he or she is actually packing it up. But I've got to say that there's a weird sense, or like a mood, while you're watching it—I can't really explain any better. A sense like something or someone is going down here, you know?

HERE'S ONE FOR YOU, miss. Though the Australian electoral system is designed to guarantee the absolute privacy of one's vote—and of course you'll well know that it's both illegal and theoretically impossible for any person to observe the filling-in of another person's ballot, or to determine the author of any submitted ballot— yet each citizen is legally bound to the proper fulfilment of her ballot. Therefore, once a voter has entered the polling booth she is both legally obliged to submit a valid ballot *and* guaranteed that her adherence to this obligation *will* not and *can*not be policed. Assuming the claim of innocence in this regard is based upon the reasoning that one can never be accused of doing so, it must be presumed that—for those citizens who would claim it to be no breach of one's civil integrity to choose to invalidate one's ballot within the polling booth—the distinction between a law that cannot be enforced, and the complete *absence* of this law, does not exist. Presumably then, for this group of citizens, civil integrity is not only socially evidenced but is in fact wholly social, in which sense the individual is limited to being an *instrument* of civil integrity, and cannot ever actually *possess* it—and this is a belief which insists that the notion of an unenforceable law is not only redundant but also oxymoronic. Furthermore, given the redundancy of said social integrity in any non-social form, a citizen enacting this philosophy presumably also believes that the legal status of the voting booth is a practical extension of an individual's absolutely private domain— indeed, of one's free will—over which there cannot be, for epistemological reasons, over and above any moral or legal reasons, any kind of government or law. Thus, for said citizens, a government's pretences to having legal jurisdiction over the actions of an individual once the individual has entered the polling booth are both theoretically and indeed actually an attempt to govern one's mind and/ or will, which notion is not merely absurd, as previously argued, but also morally repulsive, as, for example, George Orwell espoused.

So here's something I'd love to get your precious mind's input on: in a country such ours, where one is legally bound to vote under the aforementioned conditions, should then the act of invalidating one's ballot within the polling booth be described as an *a*political or indeed an *anti*-political act? And further, does the answer to this question depend upon the means of invalidation—whether one chooses to *defile* or simply *neglect* said ballot?

Let me know how you go. Dying to hear.

Sincerely.

THERE WAS THE NIGHT WHEN I was driving him home in the rain, and he made me pull into the riverside cliffs and let him out. He walked over to the footpath and pretended to take a cigarette out of his breast pocket and light it. Then he started to limp along the path—I can't forget it. It was a beautiful limp, if you can imagine that, subtle and yet total. Everything around him was grey and green and maybe a little purple—that's what Brisbane's like when it rains. I backed the car out and began following him, slowly, at a distance. I noticed that he was holding his hand up to one cheek, like he'd been hit, or maybe he was hiding something. His other hand was in his pocket, urging the leg along, the leg that was hurt or crippled or whatever. Then I noticed that he wasn't wearing shoes. I looked down and saw that his brogues were neatly placed beside me on the floor of the car, in front of his seat. I could feel something flushing in my chest. Privately, naively, I was screaming about not having my camera. Back then I was someone who tried to film what I felt.

The thing he was doing with his hand, I eventually realised, was pretending to shade the cigarette from the rain. The pretend cigarette. The rain was real, needless to say. And that's when I knew.

(For many of us—people like you and me certainly—who were born into the age of commercial air flight, a sense of awe nonetheless accompanies the take-off sequence of an aeroplane in which we are seated. This sense of awe, the true meaning of which can only be accessed by an aesthetic judgement, as in how we feel, makes an indelible statement about humans and what we call humanity. Certainly, the awe itself is not sufficiently explained or described by epochal vanity. Given that the individual has lived exclusively in the present era, and has never been without the capacity for air travel, said vanity should not reasonably manifest as awe, much as the ability to lift one's own arm is not accompanied by any particular emotion. Unless, of course, one's arm has been affected at some time by a form of paralysis or palsy. In any case, the character of the awe in question does not seem to be of a proud kind. It belongs instead to the category of discomfort, or displacement, rather than of acceptance or entitlement. It seems to be a kind of alienated or else conflicted awe, a sense of being subjected to something that is historically, but not personally, new. Which for me goes to the point of asking what we mean when we call ourselves a historical species. Let me put it another way. In five hundred years, do you still think there will be sick bags in the seat pockets of aeroplanes?

Well?

Pull over here. Please.)

I GOT UP OFF THE CHAIR in the Marseille station and walked toward the platform, leaving the folded copies of *Le Monde* and the *Wall Street Journal* behind. I clutched my book like a purse and dragged my case.

When the shoot had been cancelled, I had already booked the train back to Paris. Most of the models had vanished that afternoon or early the next day, but I didn't see any point in going back to London for a night. I stayed on in the hotel and read my book and watched television. It had been cold and windy out on the islands where we were working, and I was exhausted by the long shoots. I was about to begin my holiday, and I didn't want to run myself down and catch something out on the streets.

The concierge was fond of me, and he sent me up room service on both nights.

The first time I heard anything about it was the evening after the shoot was cancelled. I had gone down to the lobby to borrow another pen. In the elevator I ran into one of the Italian models with her bags. We'd talked the day before—her name was Monica. She said that someone had died in the apartment of some old prostitutes. One of the Arab guys. There were two of them there, two Arab models, but only one was dead.

The next morning when I went out to buy breakfast there were two Polish models in the patisserie on their way to the station. I overheard them saying that one of the Yemeni models had killed the other. They'd been taking opium in a brothel. My mother was

Polish, so I understood most of what they were saying. I hid behind a magazine by the window of the patisserie, so as not to be seen.

Then, that afternoon, I went out looking for an English second-hand bookstore. I found one a few streets back from the harbour and ended up buying *Anna Karenina*. The American girl behind the counter was talking about the Yemeni boys on the phone. That was where I heard the thing about the castration.

That night I read the first part of *Anna Karenina* and fell asleep. When I woke up the next morning and packed my bag and realised I was leaving, I felt a strange kind of responsibility to know what had really happened. It was almost guilt. I asked the concierge if he had heard any rumours, but he hadn't. The taxi driver also said he knew nothing. I eavesdropped in each of the train station's cafés, without even realising what I was doing at first. There was nothing about it on the internet either. I bought some newspapers which also didn't mention anything. I sat down near my platform and called my agent; she thought the shoot had been cancelled because the photographers hadn't gotten enough visas. Though she had heard something about a brothel, but couldn't remember what it was about.

There were not even any threads to pull, I realised. At page 194 of *Anna Karenina* I found a coupon for a complimentary refreshment from the Rome airport, dated the eleventh of August, 1979. The name written inside the front cover seemed to be Hanibel O___.

When the train arrived I conceded that I was leaving it all behind. The rumour had come to nothing; it was like I had been tapped on the shoulder, and then I had turned around, and no-one was there.

I'M DRIVING TO MY MOTHER'S HOUSE when I hear on the radio that an election has been called. It is her birthday. I walk up to the veranda of her house, which is in the dream where it is in reality, which is to say in Moorooka, Brisbane, on Clive Avenue, number 16, a big sort of place with faded red gables and a row of palms along the footpath. The election is coming in a matter of months, or so the radio said, that's where I heard it, in the car, and I know you're going to say that it's true to life, that part, that the election really was announced yesterday and that it's happening soon, and I don't know what I'll say to that exactly except that I don't even have a radio, you know, and my mother's birthday isn't for months, so not everything's true but some things are. Anyhow, on the veranda there's a black woman, a Sudanese, asleep in the white armchair. This is a woman that I really do know, another true thing, her name is Daisy, or else that's the name she's taken, and she lives with my Mum at the moment downstairs in the flat that used to be my bedroom. Daisy has a scar right down her face, diagonally, crossing her nose at the bridge, and it's as smooth as anything you've seen, so pretty and strange that you sort of want to run your finger down it like a child would do without thinking. Her eye is yellowed like a dog after a scrap, though that part I guess is not really in the dream since as I said she was sleeping when I walked past, I remember that as clear as anything. Inside the house is just the way it really is, only the sense of transience, that sort of sharehouse feeling that my mother's house has always had, that's not really something

I notice when I walk in there, not in the sense that I look over at the torn and burned couches, or step in something that's not been cleaned up properly, or look over at the TV that's sitting on a milk crate in the corner of the room, or the filthy blankets scattered around the place, the fan that hangs from the ceiling on a troubling angle. Instead I just sort of move toward the kitchen without seeing anything in particular, dragged through the space in a way, everything blurry, until I'm right there, standing behind her as she reads at her tiny little circular table, dwarfing it really, and with her hair as ever tied up in a floppy bun like a Sumo wrestler, the light through the windows making the grey glow around her like a halo. When she turns around it is so slow that I think about the fact that if time stopped even for a moment, everything would be accounted for. This is the thought that hangs on through re-entry; I wake sweating and tormented by guilt.

OKAY HERE GOES, PUPPET, a summary of what I was saying in the quadrangle yesterday. A single thought of mine, subdued and restrained, so that you can take your little scalpel to it. It is my pleasure.

In the future there will be completely new *brands* of curiosity, as in people will want to know things that they've never even thought about until now. They will ask a question that it is not yet even *possible* to ask, not today. Even the nature of this question will be completely new, the very nature. All that can be known about the question now is that it is inevitable, or else that's what I'm all about trying to explain to people. It is inevitable in exactly the same way that it is inevitable for a machine to make errors that do not seem like errors, errors which make the machine seem *intelligent*. And there will be no-one to blame for this because the question will be anonymous in the purest sense—a meaningless outburst mistaken for language—which, once the mistake has been made, will seem like a medium by which it has become possible to publicise some entirely personal, yet eternally constitutional, part of the human experience (humanity). And here's the thing: there will be no ethical way to ignore the question, once it has been asked.

If it helps, you can think about this new kind of morality the way an evolutionist thinks about mutations. As fortunate accidents. Convenient error.

Any problems, you know where to find me.

Sincerely.

(MY CONCERN IS THAT there is some kind of technology available to everyone by which it is possible to know exactly where my eyes have fallen, like there's a sort of ocular fingerprint that I'm leaving everywhere.)

'Chapter 9 ("Minor Works, Undisputed"); Part 2 (Lecture Series, June – August 2020: "On the Brink of the Brink"); No. 8 *On David Gould*'

So yes, amid the decade-long flurry of output following her self-realisation as an unlikely cultural figure, until her still quite recent death, she prefaced two of her books with a quote attributed to one David Gould, an otherwise wholly unknown—and indeed, un*verified*—South Australian poet. The disputed Gould's disputed writings were never formally published, nor have they appeared in any fashion prior to the infamous, seven-page essay slash tribute slash experimental narrative in discussion here and now, whose factual basis has proved a veritable bigfoot for academics such as yours truly, thanks largely of course to the elusive nature of our subject.

Ladies and gentlemen I welcome you again to what I suspect you are now beginning to notice is a seriously well-trodden garden path.

It goes without saying that she is Gould's only biographer, if not the imaginary Gould's creator. Whatever the case, it is through this quotation that she introduces us to him, for the first time, formally:

> *All I know is that there are seams*
> *and that it has to be perfect is true.*

Which may or may not be a very simple rhetorical joke. And for the sake of your sanity and not to mention the plausible duration of this lecture, you might as well assume for the time being that it is. Or else just don't think about it for the next twenty minutes.

In this essay, broadly speaking, she depicts Gould as a kind of part-Dadaist, part-Socratic. Ostensibly a poet whose subject is the tactile nature—the material reality—of artistic media.

Some of my colleagues, including most notably Mister G.B. Hitch, have argued with a certain confidence that Gould really was an invention, indeed very specifically conceived as a proxy for the inevitable re-modernist critique of her later "Yellow" phase novellas, a kind of pre-emptive battering ram and or straw man. This is of course only satisfactory to those who are happy to describe her as a re-modernist or even an ultra post-modernist, schools to which I again insist that I do not belong. I remind you that to date all arguments that accuse her of genuine engagement or even slight interest in academic and or critical analysis of her own work have lacked premise. And I will also say now for the hundredth time, and with apologies to those of you diligent enough to have been in attendance on each prior occasion, that as far as we know she has not read a single word of text besides her own since her abandonment of formal education somewhere in the mid-90s. In any case well before publishing her first known work. And yes you may refer here to my own pre-professorial paper, "ATROM" [EDITOR'S NOTE: "She Wasn't There: A Teleological Refutation Of Metacognition"], for flawed but not entirely useless fleshing-out of this argument.

Please note here that the theory that she lived after a certain time in a strict intellectual and cultural vacuum is not uncontroversial. Actually, you might as well underline that point and use your highlighters and red pens in such a way that I cannot be accused of brainwashing.

What is not controversial, however, is the fact that there are no original Gould texts to be found. Gould—whether a fictional character or real, historical, human entity—did not write his work down, but rather recited it from heart at small gatherings. When he read out his poems he wore stockings on his head and was naked from the waist down. She describes, with unusual poetry, "the shrivelled bunny ears that were his frame and parenthesis... the swinging flesh that kept his time." According to her, he was a terribly nervous person who spoke, quote, "in smeared falsetto." His followers, on whom she casts but a brief, fleeting beam of torchlight in this essay, were evidently few in number, mostly women.

She notes, without elaboration, his many poems about vinyl records. It is here that she alludes to his participation in an underground gothic culture associated with the heavy metal music scene in the eastern suburbs of Adelaide—a tempting research path many have followed, albeit unfruitfully. But the bulk of Gould's poetry has as theme and topic the act of reading books. Four whole pages of *On David Gould* are dedicated to a single poem, which in popular and probably irrefutable criticism is considered fairly immature. She makes a point of saying that what is quoted here is subject to her memory and—those of you who smell a festering rat in this little house of mirrors will enjoy this one especially—quote, "ought not be mistaken for the original."

In any case, the poem as recorded:

Snake.

Aiming from desert rock to desert rock,

Belly sweeping wild over sand.

But moving.

Eyes gripping jagged letters, crawling madly across stanzas,

Idle stupid drifting distracted in the blanks.

But progressing. Up and right.

Clearly enough—and you'll just have to excuse all the slippery prepositions here because of the certain doubt in which anyone studying this particular work is inevitably suspended—most of these poems describe the physical and or psychological and or spiritual disposition that converts ink and paper into stories, ideas, and what-have-you. When reading, Gould notices, we tend to look up or else blink as we turn a book's pages, convincing ourselves that a page has no depth and is, somehow, directly commensurate with the immaterial nature of our imaginations. We *fool* ourselves, as a means of understanding, or believing. And this self-delusion is not just a means to an end but perhaps in fact *who* we are, in a bigger context.

He goes on along the same tangent in a subsequent work. Here, perhaps, a little more crankily. Evidently and of course, the author's vanity does not quite catch his own attention:

> A book is a monad is a spine.
>
> Gloss, kind, illustrate, sell, sold, lined.
>
> Long library. Truffle shelved.
>
> The critical third,
>
> Dimension.
>
> Time, it demands two thumbs of me.
>
> Terrible habit asks: how much has my mark moved tonight?
>
> This seamless world. We insist.
>
> For shame we are,
>
> Abstract pathetically.

The bewildered and angered tone in which Gould describes this phenomenon will be fairly familiar to those of you looking back at your early twenties. This is, by appearances, a nigh-on precisely stereotypical introduction to the intellectual scratching of an existential itch. The first clumsy, baby-elephant steps of philosophy. Angst, by another name.

In her own proactive analysis of these two brief poems, she describes a sitting man with a giant phallus and a mouth that gapes and sucks on its tip, forming a sort of human loop or else—and I borrow a phrase that's probably more cute than useful—"infinite masturbation." There is a book on the man's lap and he is reading it and he is weeping or else choking on the phallus. And the man has giant ears that droop—though not like a bunny but, quote, "like giant petals or fronds lightly parted to sun his face." There are no surprises here, neither for us nor for her; we see Gould with a condescending glare, amazed but neither surprised nor particularly impressed as he takes the routine steps of self-knowledge.

In an unquoted poem entitled "The Stubborn Mirror," Gould apparently speaks about the experience of reading a series of books continuously for three days, without sleep or food, but all the while ensuring that he forced his eyes' focus to move deliberately and carefully onto the edge of each page as he turned it, pausing for seconds and sometimes minutes to pay utmost attention to the fine point of near-nothingness that separated the words on one side from those on the other, thus defying or else attempting to defy the aforementioned "fooling" of himself. A sort of Brechtian exercise, as it was described in my own time. His poetic image, she claims, was that of a spider or else a bug on one's hand, which, as one turns one's hand over, must travel over the thumb or the forefinger's edge, and indeed balance there if the hand so pauses. This poem, she cryptically wrote, was perhaps "the most disturbing thing I had ever read while I was a spider." Besides the opening quotation, this has proved by far the most discussed aspect of *On*

David Gould; it appears to some to service the titillating question of whether she was a morally good person, and a photocopied page with these words highlighted was famously mailed to a number of past Nobel Laureates when she was a serious candidate for the prize. It is today more often than not misquoted—the words "had ever" routinely omitted. I'll point you to at least ten examples of this from scholars who should know better, in my notes.

Of final note, in the extended preamble she excuses (in a tone of undoubtable sarcasm, needless to say) the unconventional structure of her tribute, which has no discernible introduction, and which ends in a flurry of unpunctuated onomatopoeic words. But her excuse is of course its own pregnant riddle: "a guide in this sense is truly a slave; leave me if I am strange, and know that it's true."

The question you might be asking is whether Gould is or was real. Perhaps I should slap your hands and tell you that you should really know better. But instead I'll assure you that we all want to know the same. To give you a hint as to the general tone of things, as far as I know only once has a serious critic treated her essay as a genuine biographical text, and thereby written of Gould as a real and actual historical being who is probably still alive. Indeed, that critic—again, I will reference in my notes—quickly dismissed the few examples of Gould's work, as we have essentially done here, as petulant and without much poetic merit. Also as pretentious, angst-ridden, and ultimately inconsequential. In which sense, perhaps, the claim that these poems comprise a coming-of-age document is arguably perfect to the point of redundancy, or myth.

Of those of us too embarrassed to speak of him as though he were real, most argue, perhaps in frustration, that her invention and or celebration of Gould is deeply cynical. Maybe her most unsympathetic work. And though I personally can't let go of Gould's possibility altogether, on which hope I'll elaborate, I do tend to agree that *On David Gould* is a spiteful piece of literature. In fact, more than one feminist critic has described it as a generalised revenge piece on behalf of the entire female sex, but I'm not going to gratify that, for more reasons than the blindingly obvious one.

I have personally given years to this work. I have dreamed about its subject. And for lack of a more concrete intellectual reading, I'll tell you something personal, and perhaps unprofessional, because it seems the only reasonable substitute for a firm analysis here.

When I was a student, I met a man once who wore a shirt with the name Dane printed on its front and who sat down beside me in the campus cafeteria and ate a sandwich very quietly. Once he was finished, he recited a poem about a man who takes a woman to the cinema. I don't remember it by heart, of course. But the story is roughly this. The cinema is empty. The man puts his hands up into the projected light during the movie and makes a shadow on the screen in the shape of a dog's head. The woman, who has been enjoying the movie, laughing in a restrained way, now bursts out laughing, reaches over and puts her arms around the man. That's how the poem ends. At that time I was studying Proust and to me the poem was coarse and had almost no value of any kind—the strangeness of the man who recited it and then walked away was all I noticed. But even that was a fairly fleeting curiosity. Back then college campuses were a place of frequent eccentricity. In any case I certainly had no idea who David Gould was. When a decade later I read *On David Gould* for the first time, it held a strange familiarity. I am not saying that I met him. That's not the point. Not at all. All I'm trying to demonstrate is that I was not kidding when I said that this—what we are doing now by trying to understand—is a walk down the garden path.

Another true anecdote you'll find if you dig hard enough into my diaries: my first wife left me over a pair of flesh-coloured stockings. Which were not hers. Which she found.

By way of conclusion: my latest theory is that, rather less glamorously than most of us hope, Gould was real and perhaps her lover for a while. There are clues if you go looking. His "swinging flesh." The giant phallus. At one point she describes him as smelling "vaguely of the stuffy house, and specifically of the sparse, little bedroom that he occasionally left to see us." Perhaps she never cared much for his ratbag poetry, but she knew how to make fun of her own libido. In a way that, let's say, Arthur Miller could not. How to parody her animal passion. Sex is to intellectual analysis as chocolate is to philosophy, as they say. Because the hardest thing to do is to subtract from a reading of Gould's work the value that her gaze confers upon it. Maybe the error we're all making is to imagine that there has to be some prevailing reason that Gould inspired her. Something that endures on a cultural level. As though it were not possible that he was just some *guy*. A person, incidentally a poet, that was simply *there*. Indeed perhaps artistic merit was not the grand criteria for those who may have briefly celebrated or else endured him until his little documented disappearance.

Of that she writes only, characteristically, which is to say frustratingly and wonderfully: "He disappeared."

Dear,

I'll do better than to tell you about a dream I had. I'll tell how it was to have this dream. But not before telling you how it is to recall having had it. Everything is everything:

How, I have always asked myself, after the fact, did it ever seem other than essentially diluted? Months and then years later I would try to grab at what I had learned again to believe, but always more fully failing, as though snatching with my giant, crude hand at a jet of ink expelled by a squid in the sea (a small squid long ago fished). A maritime thing, the torn backseat wet and smelling of scales.

I woke on the Sunday with a strange understanding or else a conviction of some kind. And this knowledge, which I settled on completely, was like opposing ocean currents. I felt them each, but they kept me still. I rode in a taxi (have I ever taken a taxi in the daytime?) to your house. There was a way that I listed, leaving the yellow cage. And how the driver sped off, ignorant of my hand, outstretched. Cashless, but full of sea and weed.

Not impossible, no. I kept thinking.

And woke as though thirsty to go inside.

A man on a boat in the middle of nowhere, thinking only of water.

Seeing only water.

This is how it is to imagine myself in your eyes.

Sincerely.

I TOOK A BUS TO the very tip of Australia, which, if you know it, looks like a finger pointing north. And then I swam or else I took a small boat, or a chartered aeroplane, to Indonesia. I moved up through Asia like an urgent wind, with my head down, stopping only to eat and to sleep. I grew filthy from travelling. Where was I going? Toward my fate, that's all I know. To here, I suppose. I remember nothing of it really, no emotions, nothing aesthetic, aside from the burning sensation inside my nose, since I only had the one nostril at the time and every frozen breath I took came through it. I ran with my mouth shut. One night on a field in Vietnam I stopped to sleep inside an empty cottage or else a hut. There was nothing inside and no-one around. I was woken by deer looking in through the open windows, bleating, or else making some kind of terrible sound. I got up and left, shoving aside a huge doe that was blocking the doorway. I remember the meaty feeling of my shoulder as it drove into her chest, throwing her back a pace. I was not followed. I moved on. It went on forever like that. Then one night I was chased along the Indian border by a pack of children or else very small people wearing masks, which was like the subcontinent itself anthropomorphising to capture me. I was caught and thrown over the back of a motorcycle and driven into a cave in the side of a mountain. There a woman with layer upon layer of ruffled skirts and nothing to cover her breasts tried to talk to me in a language I didn't know. Then she used a language I did know. She asked me what it would cost to make me leave the East forever.

I realised that she was frightened of me, but I also understood that she was obviously the bravest of people, and that that was why she'd been given the task of bargaining with me. I don't remember answering her. Instead I woke up with a new face, which is to say as another person. I was in Peru, in civilian clothes, in a market, and there was a Japanese girl trying to talk to me. I didn't understand her. Not then, nor ever. But anyway I took her hand and made her my own. After Peru we moved to Argentina, and then to Colombia. (We spent too long there. That's the truth of it. Not that I want to say anything bad about the city, or Colombia, for that matter. The fact is that I don't know the first thing about either of them— that's *exactly* the problem. For a while I couldn't tell what was happening because I was happy and that was something new for me. We took the bus to a hotel in Melgar one weekend. But as we came down the mountain and passed through the little towns on the way, I saw a kind of fear overcome her that didn't really subside until we returned to the city a couple of days later. We stayed on in Bogotá until the end of the year, travelling to the coast a couple of times because it seemed to please her. We hadn't made friends with a single soul in over five months. Nor had we been apart, except in our dreams. That is, unless she was following me in my dreams, as I once suspected. Though there was the one week when she flew home out of Cartagena, and I waited for her in this old woman's apartment, wondering if I'd ever see her again. That was a week of unbelievable anxiety. I pretended to be someone else, an artist, and I almost went crazy. I probably would have kept the alternate personality if she hadn't returned. I have nothing to offer artistically but I'm better at lying than anything else. On Christmas Day of that year a man stopped us as we were walking to the supermarket near our hotel. He asked where we were from. He was English and had lived in Bogotá for ten years. He owned a restaurant not far from the hotel, on the edge of the Candelaria district. He invited us to a New Year's Eve party at his restaurant. On the night she dressed in a strange green dress that I'd never seen before. She put on makeup for the first time since I'd met her. Her lipstick and eyeshadow drifted across the lines of her face, as though she was a child who'd stolen her mother's toilet purse. When I saw her smiling to herself in the mirror, I grew incredibly nervous and for a while I tried to get her to forget about it altogether and to convince her that we should stay home after all. I failed. We went to the man's restaurant at dusk. There were metal grilles around the front of the building like a cage. No-one was inside and all the gates were padlocked. We walked around the back to the courtyard and jumped the fence. The back of the restaurant was basically the same as the front, enclosed by vertical bars. There was a window cut into the back door. Standing on our toes, we could see that there was a table set for a party inside. There were candles burning across the table and paper crowns on each of the chairs. The plates in the middle of the table were piled with food that looked like it had just been laid out. There was no-one sitting there though. We called out and knocked on the door through the bars, but no-one answered. We sat out on some plastic chairs in the courtyard and waited. After about an hour she started sobbing. The makeup streaked down her face. She went back again and again to the door and screamed to the man, whose name I've somehow forgotten now, or else I've probably blocked it out for my own good. Her voice cracked and slid horribly when she screamed. If you've ever heard a soft-spoken Asian woman howl, you'll understand. Eventually I went up and put my arm on her shoulder. The candles continued burning inside. I told her to sit with me but she wouldn't budge. She screamed again and again and shook herself against the metal bars. At eight o'clock or so the next morning, she woke me up in the plastic chair. On our way out I looked inside again. The food was still there but the candles had exhausted their wicks. We climbed the fence and walked back to our hotel.) We went to Panama and then to Mexico. She spoke very little English and I spoke no Japanese, and neither of us understood more than a word or two of Spanish. We hardly left the hotel rooms where we were staying, and most of the time I suppose we might have been anywhere on earth. But, no, that's not accurate. We were alone and we were nowhere, which is not true of too many places. We'd stay in one place until I woke one day and recognised what I saw, felt something like belonging, and on that day we'd prepare to move city again. In the absence of exercise for my one and only language, without any friends, nor books or magazines or newspapers, which I'd deliberately banished, I felt something like liberty, a clearness of thought, or else thought-lessness. We made love all through the days. And the nights, until sleep crept up and swallowed us. Sometimes we'd fall asleep in the act, one or both of us. Years later, when we no longer shared anything but the past, I read by chance through a catalogue of sexual intercourse and discovered that we had been driven, by instinct or else sheer isolation, to the very bowels of depravity in those days. I had never thought of our lovemaking as a series of actions that could be isolated, described, and labelled. But I have learned that certain things we did are considered among the more marginal acts of sodomy. By which I mean the *outer* margins. I can only suppose that this was a consequence or else a coincidence borne of our absolute ignorance. In any case, those were the acts through which I consider my adulthood to have begun. It was only through them that I truly became someone other than myself. Or so it seemed to me.

Dear,

Have you seen that Godard film *Contempt*? I have. I watched it last night. It's very good. Most of his films are very good. One of your doleful looks reminds me of Anna Karina, from another Godard film, one of the black and white ones.

But I realised something and that something is surveyed here:

If you think that you feel contempt for somebody, it is probably only dislike that you really feel, or else spite. Contempt is something that you *impose* upon somebody, over a long period of time, or by a million subtle and innocent gestures that mean nothing in isolation. Contempt is non-narrative and complex. It's almost impossible to say that it's *intended*. It is the water that you allow, through passivities (is this a word?) like laziness or ignorance, to slowly flood the house and rot its every foundational fibre. I know nothing of contempt, really. The real truth is that I think that you are doing your best to like me.

On the other hand, I'm doing a *bad* job—of writing this letter, yes, but also of other things.

People like you and I have at least one thing in common with everyone else. We don't know how to exercise contempt.

Another thing:

Professor Richards gave a lecture the other day on *On David Gould*. I noticed that you weren't there. This, too, is haunting me. And I'll tell you why. There is one particular phrase in the English language that I find concerning: "to write you"—in the sense that it is used for the same purpose as "to write *to* you." I keep coming across this phrase lately, in books and movies, and it always causes me a kind of despair. (Though I believe it's mostly an American usage.) To me, the phrase "I am writing you" can only be a biographical assertion. It means "I am creating you, or recreating you, through the act of writing." It is similar to a portraitist's statement: "I am painting you." That's the only way I can understand it.

So here's what I realised last night, after watching that Godard movie, and pondering Professor Richards' lecture, and thinking of your attitude towards me, and then wanting to know why I keep seeing this upsetting phrase wherever I look:

Given that writing and reading are the reflection of each other (like throwing and catching, speaking and listening, or—for your own purposes—filming and viewing), the phrase "I am reading some-one" (for example, "I am reading Günter Grass at the moment") must imply a kind of *un*creation (*anti*creation?) or else negation (obliter-ation?) of the subject. In any case it seems to imply the *end* of the subject (which in this case is the author), or at least the end of the re-creation of the subject (which must be the book itself).

So then, it's the end of one of us at least.

Sincerely.

I ARRIVED AT THE AUTHOR'S HOUSE well into the night. My driver, who was familiar or else fond of the area (which was not far from Adelaide, on the edge of the town of McLaren Vale, just where the hills meet the gulf), illustrated the surrounds for me, now virtually black (even my good eye is not the best, and I am hard of seeing at night). In fact I must have accidentally exaggerated my mild disability, as he took me by the arm and walked me toward the stairs leading up to the house.

We are surrounded by vines, he whispered, in a voice of false or else practised cadence, the voice of a theatre performer delivering a monologue. He must have been Greek or Italian. His touch was very selfless too, that of a certain type of man.

If you look out here, he said (and here he turned me so that I could feel the earth's tilt revolve under my feet, and I knew we were on a mild slope), you can see them running in lines that are almost forever. Corrugations of black on a heavier type of black. Like bookshelves in an infinite, open-air library. Or else almost infinite. And the water is out there (and here he took my arm and pointed it, southwest), perhaps a kilometre. Perhaps more. Perhaps less.

Even for me, he said, it is difficult to tell distances out here. By now the playacting was making me feel uncomfortable, and so once the driver had walked my suitcase up the porch steps, I told him to go. He asked if I would like him to ring the bell, or knock on the door, so that my hosts might receive me. I told him not to bother, and waved my hand dismissively, with the impatience of an old man, or else the lofty dignity of a blind one. The car (it too was black) turned slowly (its lights swept across me like a scanner) and headed out and disappeared between a row of trees, like a gleaming, wet orb that dissolved into the parched atmosphere. A minute or so later, I saw it again as it entered the main road in the distance, then disappeared truly over the valley's far side.

I sat down on the step, rested my case between my legs (the three books—alone, and far too well accommodated—moved hollowly and distantly, like something hitting the bottom of a well), and I combed my hair.

I first heard of the election that afternoon, some three or so hours ago, on my way to the airport. Though it hadn't registered truly at that time. My mind was adrift, preoccupied with my assignment, such that the announcement over the radio had happened somewhere at the periphery of my attention, out where the memories of the colours of a room, the tune of background music, and dreams that don't immediately wake a sleeper are held. The word subconscious may be useful. Though personally I believe that discussion of the mind is never more than a spiritual exercise.

For the week leading up to my assignment, I had been dreaming about my mother; I am driving to her house, I walk up the steps to the veranda, I enter the house through the lounge room, I walk into her kitchen and I see her from behind. Though these facts are true in every version or else episode of the dream, the dream is subtly and indeed definitively different each time, so that the overall effect is less that of a recurring dream than a cubist one, gradually built and experienced over the many nights of a single week. The purpose of the dream is of course a mystery to me, or else it had been until now that it occurred to me to think of the announcement of the election as a snake (and doing so, I felt again the guilt of a child):

When I was five years old, I was lying in the hammock on our veranda, dozing, and a snake moved soundlessly through the jamb of our kitchen door. From where I was lying, across my chest, I could see the snake clearly. And today I have distinct (though no doubt mythologised) memories of its slow passage inside. The strange thing is that I would also argue that I hadn't really seen it. That the snake, like the announcement of the election over the radio this afternoon, existed somewhere at the periphery of my attention, in the blurry corner of the consciousness wherein things are registered without value, a place behind infinitely thick glass. The kitchen was my mother's domain; for all my life she spent most of her time there, working at a small circular table by the window. Our cats spent their days around her feet or on the window sill. I cannot say definitively that I always despised her (that my resentment of her began before my father's death), nor with enough confidence that I would have meant her harm. But the indisputable truth is that I watched a snake slip into her space and did nothing to stop it or alarm her.

The circumstances of this small, quiet decision were profound. My mother, impossibly, was not at her desk at that time. A squeal came tearing out of the kitchen and I raced to the window (that I already knew the cause of the scream is probably incriminating) and to my horror my father was standing at the far side of the room, jumping up and down with his massive weight so that the floor- boards were actually cracking. I had never known my father to be afraid of anything; a giant rugby player with a curly, silver mous- tache, he was of course my very image of security. I watched him from behind glass as he smashed against the kitchen bench. Shelves cracked and spat splinters, while plates fell and shattered as he attempted (irrationally, though not without some success) to stretch the space that bound him to the snake that I had let in. The squeal- ing persisted mercilessly, of such a high pitch that my ears rang long after the incident. Eventually he ran up against a window that led out to our yard, and his massive, bare shoulder smashed the glass and he began to bleed all down his side. It was through the same window that, eventually, he jumped, breaking his leg.

My father would die in a car crash a few years later on our way to the rugby club for an annual presentation. In the passenger seat (my mother would never have been seen at the club) I was nursing a small box of engraved, triangular trophies. That I spent most of the trip in fascination with the sharpness of their points, pressing my hand down upon them (and inspecting my palm, tempting the skin) as a test of my own tolerance, would have its own unpleasant albeit poetic realisation in my disfigurement.

I turned and looked at the glass doors behind which the author was awaiting my arrival; the many loose threads of my thinking were enough to make a heavy psychological blanket (and for a while I wondered if I'd ever get to the door at all, or if I would die here, on the stairs, attempting to "gather my thoughts" as they say). Behind me a plump cactus stood in a ceramic bowl and an overturned metal barbeque showed its charred wire ribs. There was a small mound of coal and a school of soot that a mild, swirling breeze was pushing about the deck.

MAYBE I'LL PUT IT THIS WAY for you. It's like a drug you don't know you're taking. Like silent music. Inert gas, leaking. She curls up in a small 's.' You can rake her hair gently around her ear. You can watch her eyes' whites and her blink milk. Her brittle wrists in a thin cuff. Her jumper's wool, nagged. A parting stitch across a shoulder's bone, to finger. She's remembered something about everything. She knows everything's ending. She always knew; everything's always ending everything.

If I've ever meant Sincerely, it is now.

I, ERROL PETER FRANCIS DOYLE, who missed the war for temporary blindness, who beat up returning soldiers in dancehalls and bars as a way of redemption and excuse, who lived with his mother until her death, who for seven years had made a model of every building and street of Adelaide, starting from the exquisitely true centre of Victoria Square, and had grown it as far as Portsrush and South Roads, as much as my parents' bedroom could contain, and whose romantic history was a document of a first cousin and two prostitutes, had finally become alienated from these thick bones and this grudge, cursed to sit as set, and to notice little. And for my last living image I had through the glass before me the backs of twenty white-haired heads, a hazy background of primary-coloured lights over a city I knew with the intricacy of a fingerprint, and soon enough one solitary face, that of Ms. Flannery. With her image in mind and your presence on my conscience, my dawdling spirit has turned over the packed earth that lay across my heavy-footed life, retold what was forgotten. When first Ms. Flannery came to the home, we used to sit together and sometimes we spoke, and covetous as I was (at that time I had a few faculties) I tried many times to make her my last erotic subject—to show me a breast, to let me touch her, or to have her touch me in the bathroom. I was unsuccessful, and gradually we both withdrew into worlds of crowded isolation; I, losing authority over my person, and she, losing her mind to a book and to an irrational and infinite way of reading. Tonight was an exquisite torture: amid the gentle utter of her pallid blue gown, she was coming near to me. And I was dying for a comedy of language that barely raised a sniffle. It is at your benign insistence that I have relived and untangled all this forensically, like a play staged, scripted, and conceived in reverse. An animal, a scalpel separating bones and fur from flesh. Or else a poem atomised, its pain and anguish lived and learned in hindsight. It is laid out now before us, without grace or elegance, without compassion or convenient forgetfulness. It cannot be but poked at anymore. In vain I ask again the obvious: allow them to open this door and find me.